PROMOTED:
NANNY TO WIFE

PROMOTED: NANNY TO WIFE

BY

MARGARET WAY

MILLS & BOON®

Pure reading pleasure

First published in Great Britain 2007
Large Print edition 2008
Harlequin Mills & Boon Limited,
Eton House, 18-24 Paradise Road,
Richmond, Surrey TW9 1SR

© Margaret Way Pty, Ltd 2007

ISBN: 978 0 263 20014 0

Set in Times Roman 16 on 17¾ pt.
16-0108-60399

Printed and bound in Great Britain
by Antony Rowe Ltd, Chippenham, Wiltshire

This book is dedicated to my friend
and much valued editor, Linda Fildew

CHAPTER ONE

THEY had been on the road for what seemed like forever; Marissa Devlin, her seven-year-old half brother, Riley and Riley's brave and incredibly protective cattle dog, a Queensland Blue Heeler, called Dusty. A number of times on the long trek from Brisbane, the State capital, through the fertile central plains of that vast State, the fiercely loyal Dusty, one of the most intelligent breeds there is, had put himself between his 'family' and anyone who looked or acted in the least bit suspicious; indeed anyone who had given the intrepid trio a second or third glance.

Dusty was a splendid guard dog, not to mention the fact he could *talk,* something that gave Marissa so much comfort she always invited Dusty into the think tank. Her rationale was she needed backup and some reassurance she hadn't made one huge mistake uprooting them from a fairly 'normal' life to hit the wild blue yonder. At least Riley and

Dusty were loving it. To them it was all a bit of a game. Neither of them fully comprehended the gamble she had taken.

In another life Dusty had done what cattle dogs do best, working and driving stock on a North Queensland cattle run; these days he was semi-retired, having taken on the responsible job of looking after his 'family.' Cattle dogs generally were one-person dogs. Nowadays Dusty answered to her, though he was still officially Riley's dog. Before that? Marissa's mind had to shut down on that one. There was simply too much pain to go there. The past had to be shoved away—although wasn't the past always there inside her, much like her heart and her lungs? But she had to focus on what lay ahead.

What lay ahead, came up on cue; a signpost, so weathered it could have dated back to a prehistoric time, listing destinations she had never heard of, let alone could get her tongue around.

Appilayarowie? Balukyambut? Cocatatocallen? Aboriginal and why not? This was Dreamtime country. From the severe cant on the signpost she didn't think the directions would be very reliable. It would work just as well to pull a blindfold over Riley's eyes and ask him to point.

Where's your sense of adventure, girl?

She was hoping to find it the very next day. At the moment her anxieties were outweighing her positive feelings.

A stand of many trunked gums were coming up on her right. Time for a break. Her arms were quivering from the time she had spent holding the wheel. She drove the utility-fire engine red with a painted black panther at full stretch on the driver's side—supposedly a bonus according to the car salesman—off the endless Outback highway, and parked it in the shade of the ubiquitous eucalypts. She had read somewhere—she sometimes thought she could win a prize for trivia—that eucalypts, all six hundred recorded species of them, made up the great bulk of the continent's natural tree-life. Eucalypts were arguably—not in the fire season—one of Australia's finest gifts to the world.

In the heat, the gums' narrow blue-grey drooping leaves denser at the bottom than the top, were turned edge on to the sun. Scant shade or not they gave off a wonderful aromatic fragrance. It immediately soothed her much like the hauntingly sweet native boronia oil she used to sprinkle on her pillow at night. The bush had such a marvellous *smell*. It had always been one of her great pleasures to breathe in the warm *gushes* of natural perfumes; the lovely lemon-scented gums, the grevilleas and acacias, the tremendous variety of native flowering shrubs and ground covers, the crush of wild flowers underfoot. She had found nothing more entrancing than wandering the rolling hillsides around her Brisbane home, mid-Winter, early Spring, when the hills were alight with golden wattles, mile upon mile. Wattle was the national floral emblem and she adored the fragrance, but it had always given her cousin, Lucy, hay fever. Not that Lucy would have joined her in her wanderings through the splendid isolation anyway.

They were well into the great South West of the State, the *real* Outback. It was almost like driving onto a new planet. One to replace poor old down-graded Pluto. No wattles here, but a burnished yellow ocean of Spinifex that went a long way towards concealing the parched reality of the land-scape. The tall seed stalks glinted silver in the bril-liant, dancing light. More than once she had felt glad she hadn't ventured into this endless expanse alone. No wonder they called it the Never Never. She wasn't entirely sure the spirits of the place welcomed them. Instinct told her they were *watching*. As a consequence, primal little fears had begun gnawing at her mind. They hadn't passed a single vehicle for days to break the eerie notion they had entered not only another world, but also a different dimension.

City born and bred she was gripped by the extraordinary *mystique* of this vast, arid region. The very air was saturated with it, but she recognised the mood of the Guardian Spirits mightn't always be pleasant. She suspected, too, the magnetic *pull* would get stronger and stronger the closer one came to the Wild Heart, the dead centre of the ancient continent and who knows, maybe the heart of the world? Every day they were travelling deeper into the riverine desert known as the Channel Country, the home of the cattle kings, bordering the great Simpson Desert.

That was the reason she was out here: to land a job as a governess on one of the Channel Country stations so she could keep Riley with her until she felt he was old enough and secure enough in himself to go off to boarding school. That would take pretty much all of what remained of the nest egg her maternal grandmother had left her, but she didn't take her responsibilities lightly. Besides she was grateful to the great force called Destiny that had brought Riley into her life.

She was certainly qualified to teach. *Over*-qualified perhaps for young children, though teaching the very young was an important job. She had a Bachelor of Arts diploma, plus Bachelor of Education and had begun studying part-time for her Master's. The advent of Riley into her life had put that ambition on hold, at least for now. Saint Catherine's, her alma mater, where she had taught History and Economics to Classes 10 and 12 had been sorry to let her go.

You'll always have a place here, Marissa, if you need it. We won't say goodbye, my dear. It's good luck! And make sure I hear from you.

Marissa had every intention of keeping her promise to her long-time mentor, Dr Eleanor Bell, headmistress of Saint Catherine's who had always tried to make life easier for her, bless her! The atmosphere at school had always been much warmer than that at home. No, not *home*. Sadly never that! It was merely the house where she had lived with her uncle, aunt and cousin Lucy after her mother had died until her first year at University when she had moved into a women's college on campus; liberation and a whole lot of problems solved in one swoop; until she became aware of Riley's existence. That had changed her course irrevocably.

Marissa shook herself out of her preoccupations and stood out of the ute, stretching her arms above her head, generally limbering up. Dusty bounded down from the back of the vehicle and took off for the wide-open spaces, startling a great flock of white cockatoos, their cheeky yellow crests raised in a broad crown as they rose into the air, filling it with their harsh protests.

'Go for it, boy!' Riley's voice was slightly croaky as he called after him. Dusty cooped up for so long tore around the vast empty tract, full of joy at being able to exercise his well-muscled, sturdy body.

'Get out and stretch your legs, as well, Riley.' Marissa bent into the vehicle to pull a road map out of the glove box, taking a good look at Riley while she was at it. Riley was an asthmatic. That meant as his surrogate mother *she* suffered, as well. She always kept her eye on him without making it too obvious, watching out for the signs. The specialist she had taken him to after that last bad bout told her he would probably grow out of it around thirteen or fourteen. She prayed the doctor was right. She had his medication. They could never be without his puffer but so far so good. She was hoping the dry Outback air would be beneficial to his condition. There were many claims this was so. She wasn't in the least surprised. The air seemed cleaner, brighter, more translucent than any she had ever breathed.

Riley obeyed her instantly. He was no trouble at all, no behavioural problems. Her father had brought him up well.

'You okay?' she asked lightly, gently squeezing his shoulder. He was small for his age, all fragile bones. Riley had lived a stressful life. She suspected there were many dark moments he hadn't told her about, but somehow he had built up an inner strength and courage by the age of seven that often brought the smart of tears to her eyes. Her little brother—she had stopped thinking of him as her *half* brother—had made his way into her heart.

'Sure.' Riley smiled up at her with his radiant blue eyes. They were densely fringed by black lashes, increasing the impact.

'You sound a little bit croaky?' She knew how fast Riley's condition could deteriorate.

'Dry,' he explained, touching his throat. 'Don't you worry about me, Ma. I'm fine. I'll tell you when my chest gets tight. Can I have a drink?'

'Of course you can. There's cold bottled water in the cooler. I'll join you. Better give Dusty a drink when he comes back.'

'*If* he comes back,' Riley hooted, running off to the back of the ute. He reappeared a minute later with two small bottles of water. He passed one to Marissa before pointing to the signpost. 'Aboriginal names,' he commented. Riley knew a good deal more about aboriginal names and people than the city-born Marissa. 'Which way Wungalla do you suppose?'

'Your guess is as good as mine.' Marissa's tone was laconic. She downed the cold bottle of water like it was the nectar of the gods. 'From the lean on that post it could be back where we came from or a thousand miles down the track.'

'This is a *big* country,' Riley said proudly. 'You'll get used to it, Ma.'

There was that *Ma* again. Despite Marissa's efforts to get Riley to call her by her full first name, he stuck consistently to *Ma*. She knew what it was all about. Riley had been desperate to find a mother figure. She was it. The *Ma* stood for Mum. From the reaction in the bush towns they had already passed through she knew people immediately jumped to the conclusion she was indeed Riley's mother; another teenage pregnancy, another single mother probably on the run. A few times she had introduced Riley as her little brother but it was plain no one believed her.

Riley, of course, did nothing to help. If people wanted to believe Marissa was his mother, he was thrilled with that. She was *everything* he wanted a mum to be, as he had so poignantly told her. So that made her around fifteen at the time of conception, and around sixteen when she supposedly had given birth to him? In the normal course of events sisters or half sisters rarely took on the single-handed rearing of their siblings.

Going down on her haunches, Marissa spread the map out on the parched ground covered in heaps of bronze leaves. She couldn't put it on the bonnet of the ute. The metal was hot enough to fry eggs. 'Ah, here we are,' she said, trying to sound the seasoned Outback navigator when navigating was way down her list of skills. At least she had made sure they carried plenty of water and supplies. 'By the look of it Wungalla is a cattle station. A *big* one!' she exclaimed. 'It's about 150 kilometres northwest of the town of Ransom.'

'Why do you suppose they called it that?' Riley asked, half turning his head to keep Dusty in sight. 'Doesn't ransom mean money you have to pay a bad person to let their captive go?'

'Amazing! Is there any word you don't know?' Marissa smiled up at him, feeling a rush of love and pride. Initially devastated by the fact she had a sibling she had never known existed, Riley was a huge plus in her life. She had never received much affection from Aunt Allison or her cousin Lucy. Riley had been ready to shower her with love from Day One. Come to that, their bonding was instant. Such was the power of *blood*.

Riley gave a guffaw that turned into a muffled sob, then a covering cough. 'Daddy used to teach me lots of things.'

Daddy! Michael Devlin, one time brilliant corporate lawyer, deceased alcoholic who had ended his days in an Outback mission shelter.

Riley's daddy, her father! How she had adored him. Pretty much like Riley who nearly eighteen months after their father's death, still cried for him at night, trying to stifle his heart-wrenching sobs with a pillow pulled over his face. She cried, too, but the tears fell silently down the walls of her heart. She thought she had cried herself out years ago, but she had soon learned tears were eternal.

Motherless Riley, was a 'thinking' boy, a highly intelligent little fellow who had physically clung to her like a drowning child would cling to a life line from the very moment he had set eyes on her walking down the corridor of a one room bush school in the North Queensland hinterland. Marissa was *family*. He had recognised her without a single identifying word being spoken. Both of them looked like their father; the *black* Irish, blue-black hair, vivid blue eyes, and, in his children's case, skin like porcelain. Riley's likely fate at that time would have been to be taken into care.

Twenty-one years of age and she had found herself surrendering to her sense of duty and the memory of the great love she had borne her father before tragedy had come into their lives, ripping them apart. Though she had known at the time what hardship could lie ahead she had consented to taking on the raising of a child, *another* woman's child, who had abandoned Riley and her much older partner, their father, when Riley was barely four. All efforts to find Riley's mother after Michael Devlin's death had ended in failure. It was as though the young woman, said to have Polynesian blood in her, had vanished off the face of the earth, leaving Riley an orphan. An orphan that is until Marissa had come into his life, never knowing, or even suspecting her father, a strikingly handsome man, had formed a relationship with a young woman he had met on his wanderings and had had a child with her.

Tragedy had shattered Michael Devlin's life, a life he had considered perfect and set him on his downward spiral; one from which he could never find the strength to pull out.

'Suicide! That's what it was!' Uncle Bryan, her father's brother had cried in great distress when finally they got the letter from the head of the bush mission, a Pastor McCauley, informing them of Michael's death and the existence of Michael's small son then in Pastor McCauley's and Mrs McCauley's care.

'Gutless!' Bryan's wife, Allison, had added in

her cruel judgemental way. Aunt Ally had no difficulty finding fault in others, but never in herself. 'Michael had everything going for him, and he threw it all away! That child isn't coming here, Bryan. I'm telling you that now. We took pity on Marissa and raised her. Don't imagine for one minute I'm going to take on another one of Michael's children. He should never have shacked up with that woman let alone made her pregnant. If they can't find the mother, the boy will have to go into care.'

Aunt Ally didn't understand grief. She didn't know much about the human condition. She had never fully understood how much her father had loved her mother. How much his life's happiness was invested in her. Then again Ally had always been jealous of the beautiful Maureen, Marissa's mother.

Yet it was Uncle Bryan and Aunt Ally who had raised her after her father had taken to the road. Before doing so Michael Devlin had set up a substantial trust fund to take care of all her expenses and see her through University, but Aunt Ally always omitted to mention that fact as though 'the raising' had involved a huge financial burden on them. It hadn't. Her father had seen to that part of his duty before he took off.

Michael Devlin had been a man full of guilt and

despair. He had lost his adored young wife in a car crash with him at the wheel. That made him in his own mind a murderer. Miraculously he had emerged with fairly minor injuries. Maureen had not been so lucky. Marissa would have been with them only as fate would have it she had been invited to a sleepover to celebrate a class mate's twelfth birthday.

Marissa, the survivor, had had to battle her terrible grief virtually on her own. The family had been devastated by the tragedy, but no one had possessed the gift of being able to offer wisdom and comfort to a child so violently and unexpectedly rendered a near orphan. Grief and guilt had consumed her father to the extent less than a year after the tragedy he had abandoned his glittering career and his child to go on his travels in a vain bid to save himself and his sanity.

The way I am, my darling, I'm no use to anyone. You'll be better off without me. At least for a while. But always know I love you.

The *while,* they had all hoped and prayed would be no more than a few months had stretched into long years. Uncle Bryan, a senior public servant, was a good man who had conscientiously tried to do his best for her in difficult circumstances. The trouble was, his wife's maternal streak was fully stretched rearing their only child, their daughter, Lucy. Bryan had loved and admired his younger far more brilliant brother, Michael, and truth be known he had always been more than half in love with Maureen, albeit in respectful silence. Lucy was two years older than Marissa. Marissa would not be alone.

Well, that had been her father's reasoning. Ten years later, not yet fifty, her father was dead from alcohol abuse. There had never been any real chance of his pulling himself together. Once he had enjoyed the perfect life with everything a man could possibly wish for. A beautiful, loving wife, a precious child, a high profile career, the grand home that went with it, the luxury cars. He had come back from time to time, suffering written all over him, telling Bryan and Ally they were 'doing a fine job.' Then he took off again, still hating himself for what he had done. Michael Devlin had been so unforgiving of himself he might just as well have committed murder.

'So how long is it going to take to get to Ransom?' Riley was asking, bringing Marissa out of her sad reverie. He bent to pat the exuberant Dusty who had briefly returned, huffing pleasurably, tongue lolling, brown eyes looking smilingly up at his owner, before haring off again into the wild blue yonder, making the most of his run.

'We're on the last lap of the journey.' Marissa rose on her long legs, ruffling Riley's thick, silky curls. He really was the most beautiful boy. How ever had his mother left him? Wouldn't that have torn her heart out? Abandoning a small child already asthmatic with a desperately unhappy, unstable, alcoholic husband was negligence on the grand scale. 'We'll treat ourselves to a tip-top meal,' she promised her gallant little brother.

'Do you think they'll have a burger bar?' Riley asked hopefully. A burger was cordon bleu stuff.

Marissa refolded the map. 'I'm certain Ransom can rise to a hamburger with chips. Hey—' she broke off, staring into the heat hazed distance '—is Dusty *herding* those kangaroos?' she asked anxiously.

'That's what cattle dogs do!' Riley, the little bushie, laughed aloud. 'They even herd *people*.'

'But the kangaroos mightn't like it!' Marissa was torn between amusement and concern. 'Dusty's a forceful little devil. Whistle him back, Riley, before one of those roos gets good and mad and gives him a kick.'

'It's okay. Dusty knows all about cattle, *and* emus *and* roos,' Riley said with some pride, but he did what he was told and whistled up his dog who came flying back towards them.

* * *

By this stage of the long journey the bush town of Ransom seemed strangely familiar. They had passed through similar towns, towns that looked like they had been there forever and would remain unchanged until Doomsday. There was hardly a soul about. The broad main street drowsed in the all powerful sun…4WDs, all with bull-bars, some of them spectacular, and covered in red dust lined the kerbs. There was a gas station, a huge open garage where a mechanic was working that obviously did repairs, a few shops, a one-man police station, a café, a community hall and the ubiquitous pub where two old-timers sat on a bench out the front. Opposite the pub was a small park, an oasis in the burnt ochre landscape.

The founding fathers had done something remarkable. They had planted a dozen or more jacarandas that had thrived in the hot, dry conditions. It was late October and they were out in all their billowing, mauve-blue glory, some forty feet high and about the same in spread. Spring-pools of spent blossom decorated the ground at their feet, turning a small bush park into a *dream* of beauty.

'Aren't the trees lovely, Ma?' Riley said, leaning against her, always hungry for the reassurance of her touch. 'I never thought they'd grow way out here in the desert.'

'They grow in the high dry deserts of their native Brazil,' she told him, giving his thin shoulders a hug. 'The dryer the year the better the show. You wouldn't have seen jacarandas way up in the tropics where you came from, more likely the poincianas, the cascaras and tulip trees. Brisbane parks and gardens are full of them all. The jacarandas would be in bloom now, but we're not missing them, are we? Someone has planted them all here. They really should be pronounced *hak-haranda*—it's much softer isn't it?—like they do in Rio. Do you know where Brazil is? Brasilia is the capital, but Rio de Janeiro is the largest city and I'm told very beautiful.' Every day she managed to get in some general knowledge, as well as taking time out for regular schoolwork.

Riley was still studying the jacarandas with enchanted eyes. 'Brazil is in South America,' he answered, as though in a classroom.. 'It's really big and the people speak Portuguese.' His tone changed into wistful. 'Daddy was the *best* teacher I've ever had outside you, Ma. He started to teach me all sorts of things when I was really little, History and Geography, spelling and writing, as well as my sums. He made everything so interesting, but sometimes he got really sick and I had to stay with Pastor

McCauley and his wife at the mission. They were so nice to me.'

'They're good, kind people,' Marissa said, very grateful to the McCauleys.

Riley nodded. 'Mrs McCauley told me I was just about the smartest kid the mission school had ever seen. I knew tons of things other kids didn't know. Daddy always spoke to me like a big kid not a little kid. He spoke differently from other people, didn't he? More correctly. He had the sort of voice you listen to, like yours, Ma. Do you miss being a teacher in your great big school?' Riley had been very impressed with Saint Catherine's, the fine buildings and the spacious grounds.

For a moment Marissa was desperate to shed tears. Instead she answered calmly, 'I have you. I'm going to continue where Daddy left off. In a few years time I want to send you to Daddy's old school. You'll find his name on the honour board. He was a brilliant student at school and at University where he won a medal. You know I'm hoping to get work as a governess on one of the stations?'

'You'll get it,' Riley said as though it were a certainty. 'You're a really good teacher and kids love you.'

'A lot of the stations would already have a governess,' Marissa warned him.

'Some might be leaving. You never know. Station children are educated at home until they're old enough to be sent off to boarding school, aren't they?'

'That's right. Usually that's around ten. The Channel Country is the home of the cattle kings. It's actually a vast depressed tract of land called a riverine desert on the fringe of the desert proper. The actual rainfall might be low but the great network of channels bring down the monsoonal rains from the North where you were born.'

'I know all about rain and the Wet Season.' Riley grimaced. 'Daddy and I got marooned once when the flood waters rose. Ugh, the mud! We had to wait for days in the truck before we could cross the bridge. Do you suppose Wungalla needs a governess?' he asked hopefully. He sounded the word out in the soft musical lilt of the station aborigines he would have come to know as a small child. *Woo-oon-gah-lah*.

'I shouldn't be a bit surprised!' She wasn't about to worry him. 'Now what about we try the café across the street. It looks clean and cheerful. Beats me why they called it the River Café. There isn't a river in sight.'

'Must be a joke. What about Dusty?' Riley immediately thought of his pet.

'We'll do what we usually do. Tie him up outside. Don't worry, I'll get him a hamburger.'

'With lots of tomato sauce. He *loves* tomato sauce.' Riley grinned. 'He'll even drink it!'

'That your dog outside?' the woman inside the café queried when she had been watching them tie Dusty up.

'His name's Dusty!' Riley answered, his beautiful little face lit by a friendly smile.

'Best dog in the world the Australian Cattle Dog,' the woman pronounced, wiping her hands on the spotlessly clean apron she wore over a floral dress. 'You didn't forget to give 'im some water?'

'Oh, no.' Riley shook his head. 'Ma and I look after Dusty. We love him. We're going to get him a hamburger with tomato sauce. Do you make hamburgers?'

'Make everything, luv,' the woman said, giving him a wink. She was as short and stout as a barrel with a pleasant face, sharp blue eyes full of a dry humour, deep sun seams fanning out from them 'Is that what you and your mum are after? Hamburgers?'

'With chips?' Riley asked hopefully.

'With chips.' She nodded. 'Sure.'

'Gee, thank you,' Riley said politely.

'Where you goin', luv?' The woman flicked a kindly glance that masked more than a touch of sympathy, at Marissa.

Marissa smiled, responding to the woman's motherly aura. 'We should introduce ourselves. I'm Marissa Devlin. This is my little brother, Riley.' Marissa extended her hand and the woman wrung it enthusiastically.

'Nice to meet yah, luv. I'm Deidre O'Connell. I own this place.'

'It's very nice!' Riley, ever the diplomat piped up. 'Why do you call it the River Café?'

'I thought it was kinda witty.' Deidre gave a spurt of warm, raucous laughter.

'It is,' Riley agreed.

'My, aren't you a sweet talker and a real little gentleman. Mum brought you up well.'

Why bother to say again Riley was her little brother? 'I'm hoping to get work as a governess on one of the stations,' Marissa said. 'You must be a community leader, Deidre. Would I have a chance?'

The newly elected community leader threw up chubby hands that were surprisingly smooth and delicate. 'Heavens, luv, you're too good lookin'. So's your boy. If you were the Missus on a station would you hire a real looker to take care of yah kids?'

Riley's blue eyes focused on Deidre with deep puzzlement, but Marissa answered firmly. 'Yes, I would. If she were a young woman of good character and proven qualifications.'

Deidre ran her thumb down over her dimpled cheek. 'Struth, luv, governesses fall in love with the boss the whole time.'

'I won't be doing that!' Marissa shook her shoulder-length, curly hair emphatically.

'No, they'll be fallin' head over heels in love with you,' Deidre retorted. 'But you need work, luv?'

'I do.' Marissa's expression was very serious. 'I am—was—a school teacher, a good one. I have references. I need to keep Riley with me for a few more years yet.'

'Reckon you do, luv.' Deidre nodded sagely, as if there was no need to explain. 'What then?'

'He'll be ready to go to boarding school.'

Deidre's mouth fell open in awe. 'Struth! That'll cost money, luv.'

'I have some set by.' Marissa said.

'Brave lass!' Deidre gasped in admiration. 'But *some* won't stretch far, luv. Happen to know it costs a fortune sending a kid away to boarding school. You're not on the run from anyone are yah? Like a hubby or a boyfriend? You're okay here. Ransom isn't even on the Atlas.'

'I'm not on the run, Deidre, but thank you for your concern. I don't have a husband or a boyfriend.'

'Yah soon will!' Deidre cackled. 'I'd like to help yah. I recognise class when I see it. Obviously you've fallen on hard times. Don't we all! Now there are stations all over the South West as you know. The closest one to Ransom is Wungalla.' She, too, pronounced it aboriginal fashion. 'Don't reckon Holt would be lookin' for a governess, though. That's Holt McMaster. His little girl, Georgia, is six or thereabouts. Right sharp little kid but real *homely,* not that I should be commenting on such things. But Holt is plain *magnificent!* His wife, ex-wife, I should say, Tara—they're divorced—was mighty glamorous but as hoity toity as they come. She made me feel like I'd just rolled out from under a rock. Little Georgia doesn't take after either of them. Aunty Lois has been staying on Wungalla for quite a while.' Deidre let her eyes roll heavenwards. 'That's Tara's sister. As I understand it, she supervises Georgia's lessons. You won't get your curly little head in there, sweetheart, if you know what I mean?'

'Oh!' Marissa let the full implication of that sink in.

'Better get those hamburgers goin'.' Deidre announced cheerfully, realigning her stout body.

'Little fella looks hungry. He wants a bit o'building up, Mum. No offence, luv. I bet you're a great little mother. Now, what would you like to drink, son? Don't say any sort of fizzy drink. Rot yah teeth.'

'An apple juice would be great!' Riley wisely settled for the healthier alternative.

'Right! Go and sit over there,' Deidre instructed. 'Take the weight off your feet. This won't take long. Bettcha like ice cream?'

Riley's smile broadened. 'Chocolate chip? That's my favourite.'

The older woman laughed and waved a hand. 'Say no more.'

They sat across from one another at a window table. They could have spread out anywhere. There were no other customers. 'Deidre forgot to ask *my* dietary requirements.' Marissa leaned across to whisper. 'She was too busy looking after you.'

'Don't you want a hamburger? Everyone wants a hamburger.' Riley craned his head to see if Deidre was listening in.

'A hamburger's fine,' Marissa said, settling back. A steak sandwich would have been better, or a ham and salad roll, but never mind. Many nights she had found a secluded spot where they could sleep in the back of the ute. Tonight she would ask Deidre if there might be room for them at the pub. It was easy to recognise Deidre was a woman of consequence.

The hamburgers when they came were everything hamburgers should be. The buns were fresh and lightly toasted on the inside, the beef patties topped with a cheese slice were extra tasty. There was also a slice of bacon, a thick slice of tomato, a sprinkle of little salad greens and a thick chunk of home cooked beetroot to give the beef a sweet tang. The accompanying mound of chips was cooked to perfection. Riley had his Tasmanian apple juice, Marissa a cappuccino with two freshly baked cup cakes while Riley polished off a large bowl of chocolate chip ice cream.

'That was simply *wonderful,* Deidre,' Marissa said, meaning it. 'It hit the spot.'

'It's the *best* hamburger we've ever had.' Riley rubbed his small stomach.

'I thought you'd be pleased.' Deidre beamed on them. 'Why don't you stick around for a day or two,' she said to Marissa. 'I'll see if I can find out if any of the station folk are lookin' for a governess. The school year is almost over, luv, but some parents like their kids to continue with their lessons right through. Gives 'em a bit of an edge when they go away to boarding school. Reckon some governesses might be leavin' and not comin' back. Yah never know.'

'That's very kind of you, Deidre,' Marissa said, marvelling at meeting such a helpful woman. 'Would there be room for us at the pub?'

Deidre gave another one of her rich belly laughs. 'I don't know whether you've noticed, luv, but it's the *off* season,' she joked. 'Pop down and settle yah selves in. Me brother Denny owns it. He's a bit deaf, but he'll hear yah if yah lucky or Marj might be around. Marj is his wife. Tell 'em I sent yah. By the way I've got some tucker for yah dog. Best dog in the world, the Queensland Blue Heeler,' she reiterated. 'Mind you some of 'em have a bad habit of nippin' at yah heels. Hang on a minute and I'll get a doggy bag.'

'How much do I owe you, Deidre?' Marissa called as the woman disappeared into the kitchen. So far Deidre hadn't presented her with a bill.

'Nuthin', luv,' Deidre responded when she returned. 'It's on me. I can see the situation is pretty grim for you and the lad.'

'Truly it hasn't come to that, Deidre,' Marissa protested, more than ready to pay and producing her wallet.

'I notice these things,' Deidre said, waving the wallet away. 'You can pay me when you land a job.'

It was the start of a long-standing friendship that began that very day.

CHAPTER TWO

How different everything looked after a good night's sleep. Marissa stretched like a cat in the ray of golden light that fell through the upper-storey window.

I've a good feeling about this place, she thought. Maybe Destiny has drawn us here. Destiny had played the leading role in her life. She slid out of bed and padded across the polished floor to the open doorway of the adjoining room so she could peek in on Riley. He was still fast asleep, looking positively angelic. In a minute or so she would head down the narrow corridor to the bathroom to take a shower. Like Deidre's café, the pub was spotlessly clean, but the rooms were very basic, fitted with a single bed—no doubles, no couples?—a wooden chair, a wardrobe and a small chest of drawers with a mirror above it. Neat lace curtains hung at the windows. There was a modest rug on the timber floor and centred above the bed, a touch of atmosphere in the form of a framed print of a caravan of camels crossing a fiery-red sand dune.

Denny and Marj, the publicans, a well-matched couple—he was deaf, she had a voice to round up cattle—acted like they had known them for ever. It had been arranged she and Riley would breakfast at Deidre's place, obviously the hub of the town. 'We'll be comin' towards the end of the rush hour then, luv!' Marj had informed them, so she had better get a move on.

Deidre, her hands working on another clean apron, saw them seated and without asking what they would like hurried back to her kitchen.

'I suppose it's going to be another hamburger then?' Riley commented hopefully, looking around at the other banquettes and tables. They were nearly all filled, mostly with station hands, truck drivers or travellers passing through.

'I hope not,' Marissa said, trying to act unaffected by so many male eyes on her.

'Deidre is a really nice person, isn't she?' Riley said. 'I'm sure she'll find you a job.'

'And she won't let the fact all the jobs are taken deter her.' Marissa smiled. 'Are you hungry?'

'Starving. *And* thirsty,' Riley said. 'This is such an adventure! Good thing Dusty likes Marj. Last time I saw him he was following her around.'

'Just so long as he doesn't nip her.' Marissa made a little snapping movement with her fingers.

'He wouldn't be game.' Riley giggled.

'That's what makes him such an intelligent dog.'

Breakfast was peach and mango juice followed by a small bowl of crunchy muesli with milk and a banana, and to top it off warmed pita bread stuffed with bacon and a poached egg. All in all a very substantial breakfast guaranteed to provide them with plenty of energy.

That's if I can get up off the chair, Marissa thought, not used to eating so much. Once again Deidre refused to take payment so Marissa *insisted* she return when the breakfast session was over to help out in the kitchen. Riley could sit at one of the tables and do his lessons.

'That's really nice of yah, luv,' Deidre said, regarding Marissa with a kindly, approving eye. 'Meantime why don't the two of yah take a walk in the park. You won't see a more beautiful sight than them jacarandas. Wouldn't have had 'em only for Holt's grandma, Mrs McMaster senior. She was the one who had the park set up. Some Pommy landscaper friend of hers planted them. The locals were ignorant of such things but Mrs McMaster is a real lady. Pommy, too, but we never held it against her. She was kinda like a lady

General or maybe even Royalty around here. She told us all what to do and we did it. Course the McMasters are Bigtime. They own the town. Know how it came by the name of Ransom?'

'Please, tell us, Deidre,' Riley begged.

A male voice in the background yelled. 'I was wondering if I could get my sausages and eggs, right about now, Dee?'

'Keep yah shirt on. I'll be right there,' Deidre yelled back over her shoulder. 'I'll tell yah later, Riley, me boy. I'm fairly certain you don't know what ransom means, but Mum will tell you.'

Marissa took Riley's hand leading him out onto the footpath. 'You'll have to start calling me Marissa, Riley. People really do think I'm your mother.'

'Yes, well, remember what I told you? You're the most wonderful mother in the world.' He leaned towards her and whispered, 'My real mummy used to hit me. Once she knocked me really hard in the chest. I think I broke a rib. Daddy was *so* angry. He called her a poisonous little bitch!'

Marissa closed her eyes. 'Oh, Riley,' she moaned. 'You've never told me that before.'

'I don't like to tell you anything *bad*,' he said, shaking his head. 'It wasn't long after, Keile ran off.'

Marissa's face went tight with dismay. 'You tell me you don't miss her, but do you, Riley? She's your mother after all. You must tell me the truth. The truth is important between the two of us.'

'I don't want to see her again,' Riley murmured, hanging his head. 'And that's the truth. Nat, one of the guys on the station, called her a 'bloody hippy' but Daddy thought Keile had gone off with him. Nat wasn't around any more. Daddy made a pile of her things and burnt them.'

'And there were no tears?' Marissa tilted his chin so she could see his eyes.

'No.' Riley shook his head. 'Daddy found a new place to live. He said he was going to pull himself together. Every day he told me how much he loved me. I never missed Keile. She wouldn't let me call her Mum. She was an angry person, Ma. If I did anything wrong she flew into a rage. After she hit me I used to curl into a ball and wait for Daddy to come home.'

'Oh, my God!' Marissa moaned, anguishing for his troubled past.

'Daddy said it was all his fault. He used to try so hard not to have a drink. He called it "the horrors." We were best mates.'

'I'm sure you were,' Marissa said, swallowing hard on the lump in her throat. 'He was a wonderful father to me before *my* mother died. We both loved her so much. It was the way my mother died in a car accident with Dad driving that started him drinking. He never used to. He was seeking forgetfulness.'

Both of them were so engrossed in their conversation they hadn't noticed that someone had followed them out of the café, until a man dressed like a station hand, caught up to them as they entered the park.

'Howdy!' he called cheerfully, touching a hand to his wide brimmed akubra.

'Morning,' Riley piped up, ever ready to be friendly.

'Mornin', young 'un.' The man's gaze flicked briefly over the child before returning to Marissa, a certain glint in his eyes; around thirty, muscular, elaborate tattoos over both arms, good-looking in a slightly brutal way, strangely lifeless grey eyes. 'Out for a stroll with Mum?'

'My *brother*,' Marissa said, keeping her tone pleasant.

'Have it your own way.' He grinned at her, but his expression wasn't pretty. 'Mind if I join you?'

Marissa took a calming breath, glad of the fact quite a few townspeople were now out on the street. 'Riley and I want to spend some *private* time together if you don't mind,' she said, feeling increasingly wary. She didn't like the look of this man. She especially didn't like the way the lifeless eyes were jittering over her.

'Really?' He mimed a double-take. 'You're remarkably well spoken for a little drifter with a kid. Beautiful, too. A raven-haired beauty with violet eyes. A bit like Liz Taylor when she was young. What brings you to Ransom if I may ask? Name's Wade Pearson by the way.' He thrust out a callused hand but Marissa unable to mask her distaste moved back, tightly clutching Riley's shoulder, dismayed to find it was trembling.

'Oh, dear, oh, dear, not good enough for yah, eh?' Pearson sneered. 'Uppity little broad, aren't yah?' His eyes continued to run insolently up and down over her body. She was wearing a fresh white shirt with just above the knee length khaki shorts that still managed to showcase her long slender legs.

'Excuse me, I don't want trouble.' Marissa was already turning away, aware his eyes were boring a hole in her back. Where, oh, where was Dusty, guard dog of renown?

Pearson sauntered after her, his grin brazen. 'And you won't be getting any if you just relax and act friendly.' Despite the grin he was injecting a sense of threat into his voice.

'But I have no interest in getting friendly, Mr

Pearson.' Marissa rounded on him, hoping he couldn't catch the anxiety coming off her. 'Please don't bother us.'

'Hell, girl, I'm only speakin' to you,' he protested, all innocence. 'Don't walk off now.'

'You heard Ma,' Riley suddenly shouted, his blue eyes glowing hotly. 'Go away. You don't want me to whistle up my dog, do you?'

'You serious, little fella?' Wade Pearson lowered his eyes to Riley shaking his head in amazement. 'Take more than you two and your dog to stand up to me. Don't get scared. All I want is to have a little chat with your ma. I've got a coupla ideas I'd like to kick around with her. We don't see a woman as beautiful as your ma every day.'

Marissa had a sense no one would ever believe she wasn't Riley's mother. 'I told you. Riley is my *brother.*'

His reaction was a coarse laugh. 'A likely story! Hell, you must've been just a kid when some dude got to yah?' He moved in closer, lifting his broad shoulders and expanding his chest, obviously believing it had an intimidating effect.

Marissa could see Riley's lip quivering. That made her stronger. 'You're in our way, Mr Pearson. *Move!*' she said sharply.

For answer he crossed his arms over his

muscular chest. 'Spunky as hell, aren't yah? I like that in a woman. Makes me wonder how much you'd fight me?'

Riley put himself between Pearson and his sister. 'Go away. Ma and I don't like you.'

Pearson leaned down and pulled Riley's ear. 'Well, *I* happen to like your ma.' His face was a leering mask. 'I think you should keep out of this, little fella.'

'You don't frighten me,' Riley said bravely, pushing back against his sister.

'It's all right, Riley.' She calmed him, drawing him closer. Her eyes had locked on to an impressively tall man who had just entered the park. No question about it, he was coming their way. Very purposefully, she thought.

The cavalry had arrived! If so, he was the officer in charge.

Even at a distance he gave the appearance of the sort of man who would command attention anywhere. Dressed much like Pearson, there was a remarkable difference. While Pearson looked rough and ready, this man had perfected the image of the glamorous cattle baron. In all probability he *was!* The aura he gave off held such authority it had the power to render her instantly calmer.

'Back up's on the way!' She gave Pearson a challenging look.

He wasn't impressed enough to turn around to check. 'You can't trick me.' He moved closer so she could smell his stale sweat. 'You don't want me to hurt the kid, do yah?'

Marissa eyed him with contempt. 'Try it and you'll wish you hadn't!'

'You're a creep and a bully!' Riley shouted, his breath starting to come hard.

'Looks like your kid needs teachin' a lesson.' Pearson grabbed at Riley's frail arm.

At the same time as Marissa pulled Riley back, a steely voice cracked out, 'Let the boy go, Pearson!'

Instantly Pearson was thrown into a panic. He dropped Riley's arm like a shot, whirling about, bravado shaken. 'Whoa, boss!' he called. 'I was just askin' this young lady if there's anything I could do to help her.'

Riley found his vocal chords again. 'Liar!'

Pearson's boss reached them in a couple of long strides, his mouth held in a tight line. 'It didn't look to me like she was interested in your offer. Get out of here. *Now.* You've got five minutes to grab those spare parts from the garage and head back to the station. We'll talk then.'

'I swear it was nuthin', boss.' Pearson held to

the role of injured party. 'She looked like she needed help.'

'Maybe you didn't hear me. I said, *go!*' The newcomer stabbed a bronzed finger at Pearson's chest.

'Sure, boss.' Pearson didn't wait a second longer. 'See you later, Riley!' He waved a pseudo-friendly hand.

'No, you *won't!*' Riley croaked after him, sounding like he was having trouble getting his breath.

'What was he saying to you?' The man looked at Marissa, waiting intently on her answer.

Now she got the full force of brilliant dark eyes; so deep they gave her the unnerving sensation of drowning.

First impression.

She must have taken overlong to answer because Riley broke in. 'He was bothering Ma,' he said, thinking this was a *real* man like *The Man from Snowy River.* He was big, strong, ready to help and the way he talked sounded like his dad. 'The one time we didn't have Dusty with us, either,' he lamented.

'And Dusty is?' The taut expression gentled as the man looked down on Riley's dark curly head. 'Don't tell me. Let me guess. Your guard dog?'

'A good one, a cattle dog.' Riley gave their rescuer a warm smile. 'Thank you, mister.'

'McMaster,' the man said, little brackets of amusement etched into either side of his handsome mouth. 'Holt McMaster and you are?' He transferred his gaze to Marissa, a brow tilted in interrogation.

She cleared her throat. Holt McMaster, who else! Here was a man who was genuinely daunting, but highly unlikely to go bothering women. More like the other way around. 'Marissa Devlin,' she said, extending her hand. 'This is my brother, Riley.'

'Hi,' he said, taking a good long look at her but in a totally different way to Pearson. Just as Deidre had said Holt McMaster was a seriously stunning looking man but very much on the stern side, Marissa thought, herself engrossed in staring at *him*. He had great bone structure—he'd probably still be handsome at ninety—hollowed out cheekbones, fine straight nose, a firm, but definitely sensuous mouth, sculpted chin and jawline. She wasn't sure if it was she or he, or maybe both of them were the cause of it, but tiny electric sparks were shooting off their momentarily locked hands.

He seemed to wait a few seconds before letting

his gaze settle back on Riley. 'Are you all right, son? Sounds like you're having a bit of trouble catching your breath.'

'He has asthma,' Marissa said worriedly, starting to rummage around in her leather shoulder bag. 'He's been fine but your station hand gave us a fright.'

'A big mistake,' McMaster responded tersely. 'You need to keep calm, Riley.' He put a hand on Riley's shoulder. 'Think you can do that?'

'Yes, sir,' Riley rasped.

'You've got the puffer?' Those fathomless eyes rested on Marissa again.

'Right here.' Marissa put the puffer into Riley's hand.

Both adults stood watching while the little boy inhaled. 'Good man,' McMaster praised him. 'You'll be fine now.' He gave Riley a nod of approval. 'What are you doing all the way out here?' he questioned Marissa. There was close enough to a frown on his striking face.

She felt herself blush. It was unnerving being the focus of that brilliant gaze. 'I'm looking for a job.'

'What sort of job?' he asked crisply.

She had a strong sense he didn't approve of her being out here; on the road with an asthmatic child. 'I'm a trained schoolteacher. I have excellent references. I was hoping to get work as a governess on one of the stations.'

'Do *you* want a governess, Mr McMaster?' Riley piped up, with touching hope.

McMaster suddenly smiled and his whole face changed. Marissa watched in fascination as the dark severity was totally wiped away. Light radiated off him like an actual aura. 'I hadn't been planning on hiring one, Riley. At least not at this time.'

'Perhaps you might know someone, some other station owner who needs a governess for their children, Mr McMaster?' Marissa asked, doing her level best to mask her awe of this man. But it was there, and she couldn't do a thing about it.

He seemed preoccupied for a moment. 'Why don't we all sit down and get something to drink,' he suggested. 'I could do with a coffee.'

'What about Deidre's?' A smile curled Riley's naturally rosy lips. 'She makes very good coffee. And hamburgers. She makes *everything!*'

'You know, you're absolutely right. Deidre's it is!' McMaster extended an arm to indicate they should all go across the street to the café.

Hope soared! Instinct told Marissa he was at least considering her situation. If so, it would be another case of Destiny at work.

* * *

'Well, look who just walked in!' Deidre greeted McMaster with the greatest good humour. 'Hiya, Holt! It's good to see yah!'

'Good to see you, Dee,' Holt McMaster responded, bestowing on her that transforming smile. 'I could do with a strong black coffee.' He paused a moment, turning to Marissa and Riley, waiting on their order. 'And?'

'We've just had a really good breakfast, but I won't say no to a cappuccino,' Marissa said. 'What about you, Riley? Are you feeling better?'

'He's fine,' McMaster said. It was almost a 'don't fuss!' 'What's it to be, Riley?'

'I don't think I could fit in another thing,' Riley said, his breathing mercifully restored to normal.

'What about you come out to the kitchen and help me?' Deidre suggested. 'Let your Ma talk to Mr McMaster.'

Marissa fought to keep her composure. How was she ever going to be able to counteract this? There was that Ma again!

Deidre put out her hand and Riley took it, going willingly. 'What about Dusty?' he asked. 'I should go check on him. He'll be missing me.'

'Don't you go worrying about Dusty,' Deidre said. 'Marj is lookin' after 'im. Marj likes dogs. She's had plenty in her time, all cattle dogs or kelpies. Now I had a kelpie one time, called Shorty....'

'Riley *is* my brother by the way,' Marissa repeated a few minutes later when they were seated in the same banquette as she and Riley had occupied for breakfast. Deidre had already set their steaming coffee and a plate of freshly baked pastries in front of them. 'Half brother, actually.'

'And where are your parents?' he asked, lifting the cup to his mouth.

His scepticism was painfully obvious. 'Dead,' she said. She wasn't all that good at hiding her grief, so she masked it with a show of long acceptance.

'They must have died very young?' His gaze pinned her like a laser.

She had to be careful here. 'Yes,' she replied briefly.

'Okay.' Clearly he thought she was running away from something. 'So where do you come from? Married, engaged, any involvement?'

She looked out the window at the blossoming jacarandas, realising she was shaking a little inside. 'I was born and reared in Brisbane.'

'Surely Riley was, too?' he asked in a dry, almost mocking voice.

She felt very much on edge yet strangely more vividly *aware* than she had ever been in her life. 'Of course.' She wasn't about to discuss hers and Riley's dysfunctional childhoods. 'I'm not involved with anyone except Riley. He's quite enough. He's asthmatic as you've seen. The dry air out here is supposed to be beneficial to asthmatics.'

He had removed his akubra when they came in the door, so now she had learned he had a fine head of hair, black and shiny as a crow's wing. It was brushed straight back from a distinctive widow's peak that lent a surprising rakishness to balance out the severity. She started to panic thinking perhaps she was giving him too much attention.

He didn't appear to notice, so she relaxed a little. 'I've seen cases of a complete cure,' he was saying. 'I don't *know,* but it seems to me Riley's condition has an emotional component. He's a fine-looking boy, but he's on the frail side.'

It was perfectly true. Even so, her blue eyes flashed. 'I'm hoping to change that. I've had him with me since our father died but it wasn't working out. I taught at a private girl's school. I often had early and after-school commitments. It was difficult with Riley, difficult to find minders. Then there was his asthma. People don't like the responsibility.'

'One can understand that. So you decided to come a thousand miles West to see if you could find a job as a governess on a station?'

'That was the general idea,' she said wryly. Did he have to make it sound as though she had applied for two seats on a space shuttle?

'But surely being a schoolteacher, Ms Devlin, you know hiring is unlikely in vacation time? It's almost that.'

She had been shooting glances at him, now she actually allowed her eyes to rest openly on his face; at his remarkable eyes, at his mouth, at his nose and sculpted chin. It was an exciting face, if a bit on the imperious side. He looked what he was, a powerful man. She judged him around thirty-two—thirty-four? 'I'd heard station folk like their children tutored vacations or not,' she said, trying to make it sound like she was one jump ahead. 'It really does pay to be ahead of the curriculum, especially when it's time to go off to boarding school.'

'Come on, you took a big risk.' He cut through to the truth.

She shrugged. 'Maybe, but I had to do it. Can you help me?'

His face assumed a considering expression. 'How old is Riley?' he asked. 'Seven? He seems very intelligent for his age.'

'He is,' she said, showing her pride. 'My father...' Her voice trailed off.

'*Yours and Riley's* father, yes?' he prompted, giving her another one of his assessing looks.

'I find it pretty upsetting to talk about—our father,' she said. His eyes had such a piercing brilliance she felt they sliced through all her defensive layers.

'I don't know your surname, Marissa.'

'It's Devlin. I thought I told you.'

'So you did.' There was a lick of mockery in his voice.

'Were you trying to catch me out at something?' she challenged.

'Like what?'

'Oh, the name of Riley's *real* father,' she said, a little bitterly. 'I repeat. Riley *is* my half brother.'

'You're remarkably alike.'

'Why wouldn't we be?'

'May I ask how old *you* are?' His gaze was very straight.

'Would you believe twenty-eight?' She felt very tightly wound. He was having that effect on her. Worse, he *knew* it.

'No, I wouldn't.' He shook his head. 'You don't look like you're all that long out of high school.'

'University,' she corrected. 'I have a B.A. and Bachelor of Education. I taught at Saint Catherine's College for Girls in Brisbane, grades

10 and 12. Easily checked out. Besides I have on my person at least in my bag a glowing reference from the Headmistress, Dr Eleanor Bell, a leading educationalist. Do you want to see it?'

'Why not?' He held out his hand, a very elegantly formed hand, darkly tanned, lean and strong, able to transmit electric charges at will.

She reached into her satchel bag and produced the reference from a zipped side pocket where she kept papers.

He took it, dark eyes hooded as he scanned the lines. 'Very impressive,' he said finally. He had the sort of voice that captivated the ear; dark, resonant, classy accent, no western drawl. 'I do hope you didn't write it yourself?'

'You shouldn't say things like that.' She didn't try to hide her little flash of hostility.

He looked deep into her blue eyes. 'Women lie about all sorts of things.'

'*People* lie.' His corresponding flash of antagonism registered. It would do no good at all to offend him. 'I was a good teacher,' she said, more respectfully. 'I'm teaching Riley as we go. I think I'm safe in saying his general knowledge for his age is remarkable. My father.' Once again she faltered.

'Why is it you begin and can't go on?'

'Pain,' she shot back, still not able to fully control

the flare of hostility, that alarmingly had a sexual component. 'Pain can annihilate. It can come at you right out of the blue. It can hit you with such force—' She broke off. 'Do you know anything about that?'

'None that I'm going to talk about,' he answered, his voice clipped.

'Then you're like me.' She glanced out of the window at the broad sun baked street.

Instead of answering, he asked another question. 'So you're twenty…three?'

'Yes.' She was so busy trying to absorb all her impressions of him, she hadn't considered what impression *she* was making.

An irresistible lure, had been Holt's first thought. A lone young woman Outback with a small child, her looks quite enchanting; soft, tender, very refined. She was hopelessly out of place. She looked like the heroine of some romantic novel, undeniably a beauty and he enjoyed beauty. Her tumble of silky blue-black curls pleased him, the vivid, black lashed blue eyes, the flawless complexion that would need a good deal of protection from the sun. Her aura had a special innocence that stirred unfamiliar feelings, vaguely tender. At the same time she was powerfully, effortlessly, seductive but seemingly unaware of it.

Though she *couldn't* be, he thought cynically. The birth of a child hadn't changed her body. Taller than average and very slender, it had a virginal look to it. But then he had heard the boy call her Ma. He had seen the way the boy looked up at her. Then there was the big age difference. Either Riley was an afterthought or Ms Marissa Devlin's teenage *mistake.* Either way she had had a hard time. But she and the boy had a valiant look. He liked that. That lecher, Pearson, had been about to add to her traumas, only he had happened along. Pearson was a good stockman but he would have to go if he ever again stepped out of line.

Marissa, for her part, had never experienced anything like his scrutiny. With his eyes on her, it was akin to losing herself. Something not easy to cope with. 'I'll be twenty-four next April,' she said crisply, in an effort to sound more professional. 'Do you think you can help me, Mr McMaster?' There was a glimmer of desperation in her eyes.

'Maybe,' he replied. 'I have a child.' His voice didn't soften.

Wasn't that a bit odd?

'Her name is Georgia. She's six going on sixty, an old soul. Her previous governesses, two in quick succession, weren't a big success. I had to terminate their services. At the moment her aunt is supervising her lessons, but her aunt's home is in Sydney. She'll want to be moving on. I'm divorced by the way.' He spoke as if his memory of his marriage was pretty hazy.

Marissa, of course, knew about the divorce, but she wasn't fool enough to mention she and Deidre had had a fairly in-depth conversation about him.

'I'm sorry,' she said. In fact she was very sorry for six-going-on-sixty-year-old Georgia, the biggest victim.

'Don't be,' he said briefly, the severity back in place. Where his deepest feelings lay she certainly wouldn't be invited to go.

Then she made one big mistake. 'How did you get custody of Georgia?' she questioned, then lifted a hand to her mouth. *How* had she asked him that?

'Simple,' he responded, his smile taut. 'Georgia's mother didn't want her. Mothering wasn't on her agenda so she moved on.'

It was her opportunity to say Riley's mother didn't want him, either, but she let the moment slip by. The past was a sleeping dragon. 'Poor little Georgia!' she breathed, wondering what else could have gone wrong with the marriage. This wasn't a man who would take failure lightly.

'I've been wrong about a lot of things in my

life,' he surprised her by saying. 'I thought mothers were programmed by nature to love and nurture their children, like some deep primal force. My ex-wife has no feeling at all for her daughter. They simply didn't bond, as the saying goes.'

'Such things happen,' Marissa murmured, critical of his use of *her* instead of *our* daughter. 'Perhaps it was postnatal depression?' she suggested. 'The syndrome is well documented. It must be hell to be at the mercy of one's hormones.'

'I thought so, too, only the condition is supposed to clear up in time. I try to give Georgia the best life I can. Her aunt Lois, my ex-wife's sister, is fond of her. She visits often.'

I bet! Marissa thought. She was ashamed of such a thought in the next second. Probably the unsatisfactory governesses had fallen in love with him, as well. He *was* very sexy. She had to concede that. The dominating, sweep-you-off-your-feet lover of an overly romantic bodice ripper. She, however, would require tenderness, sensitivity, compassion in a lover. She hadn't met a man with all of those qualities yet. That would bring a nice change to her life. She thought Holt McMaster very *tough* indeed. Tough, self-contained, utterly self-assured, an intensely masculine man. Getting involved with a man like that could leave a woman emotionally scarred.

Not a lot one could do about attraction, however, she thought. Attraction was something else again; something one had no control over. It transcended common sense. She had to give him full marks for coming very swiftly to her aid and miracle of miracles he appeared to be considering giving her a job, or at least a trial.

She waited nervously on his decision. If he said, *no,* a few tears might just roll down her cheeks. It took a lot of strength and a lot of character to be a good mother. God, she was even thinking the same as everyone else. A good *sister.*

'Okay, Marissa.' He gave her a sardonic smile. 'I'm willing to give you a trial run which may or may not work out, quite apart from the fact Georgy is the quintessential little terror. I have to be up-front about that. From time to time you'll be required to read to my grandmother whose eyesight isn't good anymore. Perhaps keep her company when she requires it. She's an extraordinary woman so you won't find it a chore. The children, Georgia and Riley can study together. The long summer vacation is coming up, but you have a point about their keeping ahead. Whether this works isn't up to you *entirely* as I've said. Georgia isn't an easy child, but she *is* smart. She's given to spectacular tantrums when I'm not around and I'm not around a lot.

Making sure Wungalla and the outstations operate successfully keeps me busy. It's a dawn to dusk job. Add to that I have other business interests that require I spend a fair bit of time away from home. You won't be required to do any domestic work. We have a housekeeper, Olly, short for Olive, who has been with us for thirty years and deserves an Order of Australia. Olly manages the household staff, part aboriginal girls who enjoy working at the Big House, which is what they call the homestead. How does that sound?' He sat back regarding her sardonically.

'It sounds like the miraculous answer to my prayers.'

'Don't think about it like that.'

It sounded like a warning. 'May I ask how much you're thinking of paying me?' She tried to appear composed and business like.

He sat back, considering. 'You can hardly expect pay until we get to know you.'

He liked doing this. 'You're joking, of course.'

'Of course.' He nodded. 'I was hoping you might smile. I'm not quite the ogre you think I am, Ms Devlin.'

Her heart started to beat so fast she might have run up ten flights of stairs. 'I think no such thing.'

'That's good, because you've been looking at me very critically.'

Oh, my God, he'd noticed! 'I certainly wasn't conscious of it,' she said, dismayed that it came out quite haughtily.

'That makes it all the more noteworthy,' he said. 'But I suppose we should get back to talking business. Full board, of course. What did you make at your girls' school?'

Marissa told him with faint trepidation. She had been well paid. Far above anything she expected as a governess.

Yet he confounded her. 'You couldn't have been too comfortably off on that, you and the boy?'

'It's good money actually,' she said, taken aback. 'You're a rich man!'

'So?' He stared straight into her eyes.

She could feel herself flushing. 'I have a little money left from a family trust. It's very important Riley receives a good education. It's my intention to send him to boarding school when he turns ten.'

'And a very laudable ambition it is, too,' he said, that maddening glimmer of amusement in his eyes again. 'There is of course the possibility you might marry money.'

Clearly he was having his idea of fun. 'Money doesn't resolve all problems,' she said in a heart-felt way.

'I couldn't agree more. Now what about—?' He

named a sum that was more than fair given that he had offered them full board.

'I'm happy with that,' she said, betrayed into giving him his first real smile of the day.

'Wonderful!' he feigned a gasp. 'That smile has taken some time!' But it was so magical it even squeezed his hard old heart. 'Now what about that dog of yours, Dusty?'

'He's a *wonderful* dog,' Marissa said, always ready to sing Dusty's praises. 'He's really looked after us. Could you possibly take Dusty on, too? He's a working dog. I'm sure you could put him to good use. Riley loves him. So do I. I desperately need this job but I'll have to turn it down if we can't bring Dusty.'

He laughed out loud. It was an extraordinarily attractive sound, one that took her unawares. 'Could you repeat that, Ms Devlin?'

'I said—'

'I know what you said. I have to tell you I find it *very* touching. You're going to *insist* I take your dog?'

'I'm afraid so.' She nodded, but her expression was tinged with worry.

'Then aren't you fortunate you're talking to a dog lover. Okay, Ms Devlin.' He put his two hands down on the table, 'I'm prepared to take you, Riley and your dog, Dusty, on board on the condition I put you and Dusty to work. Riley will have plenty of time to see him.'

So kindness did lie beneath that tough exterior! 'That's awfully good of you, Mr McMaster.'

His handsome mouth quirked. 'Whether I'm being awfully good or not remains to be seen,' he said, dryly. 'But I do like to see young people with a special attachment to their dog. People don't often confuse me, Ms Devlin, but *you* do.'

'How could *I* confuse you?' She was finding it increasingly difficult to resist the glittering magnetism of his eyes.

'To start with you're extremely out of place in the Outback. This really is the sun burnt country. You look like you'd be more at home in dewy Ireland. How are you going to protect that skin?'

'You mightn't believe this but I don't burn and I'm used to very strong sunlight.' She was surprised her voice sounded so normal when she was fighting an avalanche of sensations; all of them quite inappropriate. 'Brisbane is sub-tropical. I've coped up to date. In fact Riley and I are surprisingly sun proof. Besides, there's always sun block and a hat.'

'When you remember to wear it,' he said, looking pointedly at her bare head.

'We forgot this morning,' she explained. 'When would you want me to start?' She could scarcely credit their good fortune.

He sat back, wide shoulders squared, looking very much the Outback cattle baron. 'I suppose today makes sense,' he said. He was obviously a man long accustomed to making on-the-spot decisions. 'I'll take you and the boy in the chopper. My overseer can drive your utility back to the station. That *is* your bright red ute with the panther displayed so prominently on the side?' His mouth twitched.

'Yes.' She felt defensive, but the ute *was* hard to miss. 'I got it for a bargain. The panther was rated a big selling point. How did you know it was our ute anyway?'

He smiled. 'It's a long way from anything I've seen around here, Ms Schoolteacher.' He rose to his stunning height, his width of shoulder emphasising the taper to his narrow waist. 'Could you get yourself together in say an hour?' He glanced at his watch.

Marissa sprang up with alacrity. 'No problem!' Her mood was suddenly euphoric. She had a job. She would have Riley with her. Dusty would be looked after.

'Dusty will go back in the ute, so I'll need the keys.' His voice brooked no argument. 'It's just not possible to take him on the chopper.'

'He'll be fine,' Marissa nodded her acceptance. 'I'll explain the circumstances to him.'

He looked down on her as though what she said was preposterous. 'You're joking, right?'

She shook her head. 'No, I mean it. Dusty understands perfectly well what I'm saying. Besides I don't want him nipping your driver.'

That laugh again! 'Highly improbable, Ms Devlin. Bart is in no danger whatever of getting nipped by the likes of your guard dog. Besides, cattle dogs have an inbuilt instinct for knowing who's a friend and who isn't.'

'That's all to the good,' Marissa answered soberly. 'Because none of us can get by without friends.'

'Let's hold on to that thought, Ms Devlin,' he said dryly.

CHAPTER THREE

RILEY was thrilled out of his mind by the ride in the chopper. It was all so *exciting!* Marissa found it just as thrilling—her first time in a chopper, as well—but she managed to keep her youthful excitement under wraps. It would have taken them probably a gruelling hot and sweaty two hours to get to the station in the ute. By helicopter, they were over Wungalla, a staggeringly vast cattle station, verging into the Simpson desert, far too quickly.

A giant silver hangar was coming up. Erected on the outskirts of the *huge* station complex it comprised so many outbuildings to Marissa's fascinated eyes it looked like a world to itself. The station name and logo were emblazoned in royal blue, yellow and white on the silver roof of the hangar that looked like it could comfortably house a couple of Boeing Airbuses. Another yellow chopper, similar to the one they were in, sat squat as a duck a short distance away from the hangar, several trucks and a couple of Jeeps parked nearby.

She fully expected Holt McMaster would land the chopper on the runway, instead they kept whirring on until they were right over what was obviously the home compound, a startlingly green oasis dotted with lovely shady trees and garden beds of various shapes. It came as an enormous surprise, set down as it was in the middle of a seemingly infinite desert. She had already learned the station's longest boundary stretched for more than a hundred miles. Even walking from the airstrip to the homestead would be unthinkable.

During the flight her attention had been captured by the chains of billabongs, lagoons and water channels that crisscrossed the station like life giving veins. Impossible to believe those same sluggish waterways could rise tens of feet overnight spreading as much as fifty miles wide. This was drought country. No way of telling when the rains would come. The biggest hope lay in the overflow from the floodwaters in the monsoonal North carried down by the great western river system. Sometimes, if only rarely, the floodwaters reached Lake Eyre usually covered by a salt crust some fifteen feet deep.

The whole region was amazing. Vaulted blue skies, furnace-red earth, and in high contrast, the ghost gums—some said the most beautiful gums of all—their trunks a dazzling white against the fiery soil. It was a lonely, dramatic landscape, seemingly without borders. The authentic Australia, she supposed, its mystique celebrated in folk songs and poetry. It was amazingly easy to give herself over to it. This was a great adventure, as well as a job. She could hardly believe she had taken a few giant steps into the future.

They were standing in the driveway facing Wungalla homestead. Holt was giving instructions to a well-weathered individual who was dressed like a gardener, although a single gardener wouldn't be able to handle the workload involved in looking after extensive grounds as big as the botanical gardens, Marissa thought.

'Gosh, are we going to *live* here?' Riley's face was a study in amazement bordering on awe. 'It must be a *castle!*' he gasped.

'It's certainly very grand.' Marissa lightly shook his trusting little hand.

Wungalla homestead, begun in the 1860s and added to over the years, gave an immediate impression of colonial splendour. Lord knows how much it would cost to build today, Marissa thought. Her early childhood home, architect designed had been among the best of contemporary homes, Uncle Bryan's not quite so impressive, but this was Riley's closest encounter with grandness.

Wungalla's two-storey central section, the original homestead, was Georgian in style, flanked by long equally balanced one-storey wings, added at a later date. A broad verandah surrounded the house on three sides. Four pairs of shuttered French doors were ranged along the verandah to either side of the front door which lay wide-open. Incredibly a deep border of flourishing yellow roses ran to either side of the short flight of stone steps, not wilting but *glowing* in the shimmering heat.

Marissa like Riley stood transfixed, full of wonder and disbelief.

'Gee, I hope they like us!' Riley whispered.

'What's *not* to like?' Marissa joked, in reality just as nervous as Riley. Holt McMaster had already warned her this wasn't going to be easy.

'Right, we'll go in.' Moving briskly, he joined them. 'Hal will bring your things in and deliver them to your rooms. Though I have to say it doesn't look like you intend to stay more than a day or two.'

Marissa flushed. 'I couldn't bring too much in the ute,' she said. 'If I was lucky enough to land a job I fully intended having the rest of our things sent out.'

Those black eyes mocked her gently. 'My dear

Ms Devlin, not only could that prove to be interminable, it could blow your nest egg. Some time next week I'll fly you in to Coorabri. It's much bigger than Ransom, and it does have a surprisingly good clothing store. Western clothing, that is.'

'And what do I do for money?' Marissa quipped, intending it only as a rhetorical question.

'Charge it up to the station,' he said promptly. 'It so happens we have a pretty good clothing store here but it doesn't cater to little boys and slips of girls.'

She wasn't a slip of a girl. She was a professional *woman.* 'Are we expected?' She lifted serious eyes.

'You mustn't worry about *that!*'

'Then we're *not* expected?'

'Don't take it to heart, Ms Devlin. I wanted you to be a big surprise.' He glanced down at Riley, directly addressing him 'Go forth and conquer, Riley!'

Riley who had been smiling, suddenly looked shaken. 'That's what Daddy used to say.' His voice wobbled. How terrible it was to think his daddy was no longer there for him.

'And it was good advice! Where *is* Daddy?' Holt asked, placing his hand on Riley's shoulder.

Marissa intervened. 'I *told* you. Talking about it only makes Riley very upset.'

Holt shook his head. 'He's too young to handle

it all on his own. Haven't you ever heard the truth will set you free?'

'I've told you the truth.' Colour came to her cheeks, fire to her eyes.

'Don't flash those blue eyes at me, Ms Devlin,' he lightly warned, 'though I dare say it's relieving your feelings. Anyway, come on up. Olly is bound to be out in a minute.'

Marissa halted, to ask. 'What do we call you, Mr McMaster?'

His laugh was short. 'If you look at me like that, every man in the world might want to be Mr McMaster.' He tried it out on his tongue. 'It sounds very proper! Anyway, it'll do for a start.' He mussed Riley's hair. 'We don't want to go scaring the locals.'

A woman had come to the front door to greet them, a big welcoming smile on her face. She was in her late fifties, early sixties, Marissa estimated, dressed in a plain blue dress with white cuffs and white collar. As tall and wiry as Deidre was short and stout she had a similar look of laconic good humour.

'You've brought visitors then, Holt?' she asked, looking at Marissa and Riley with considerable interest. 'Alike as two peas in a pod.'

He smiled. 'Isn't that the truth! I must have brought hundreds of visitors over the years, Olly, but these two are here to earn their keep. I'd like to introduce Marissa and Riley Devlin. Marissa has just signed on as the new governess. She wouldn't come without Riley and Riley wouldn't come without Dusty, his faithful Blue Heeler. Riley will be joining Georgia for lessons. Dusty who hasn't arrived yet—he's in their ute driven back by Bart—is also in need of a job.'

'You're serious, Holt?' Olly flashed a glance at him, her expression comical.

'When am I *not* serious, Olly?' he appealed to her.

'When you don't care to be,' she said. Evidently she wasn't in awe of the great man. 'So, Marissa, Riley…' She shook hands with each in turn. 'Welcome to Wungalla. We haven't had a governess here for a while, but we *do* need one. Is this your first time out West?' she asked Marissa, her eyes dwelling rather worriedly on Marissa's porcelain skin.

'Yes, and we're fascinated by what we've seen.' Marissa was enormously relieved Wungalla's housekeeper was so kind and welcoming. 'I have good qualifications, Ms…?'

'Olly will do, love,' the housekeeper said, sounding very much like Deidre. 'That's goes for you, too, young fella. Now come in. I expect you'd like some morning tea, or you could wait for lunch. It's not long off?'

'Lunch will be fine, Olly,' Holt McMaster said, settling the matter. 'Meanwhile you and Marissa can sort out which rooms they want? Where's everyone?'

Olly sounded faintly sardonic. 'Mrs McMaster is in her room. It's not one of her good days I'm sorry to say. Miss Lois is out riding but should be back soon. Georgy is out in the garden somewhere playing with Zoltan. That's her imaginary friend.' She gave Riley a wink.

Riley lifted fascinated eyes. 'She has an imaginary friend? Isn't that funny? So did I. His name was Nali. He was a member of the Emu tribe.'

'So what happened to him?' Olly asked, seemingly with genuine interest.

Riley shook his head with regret. 'Nali wanted to stay with me, but the rest of the tribe wanted to go walkabout. He was just a boy like me but his uncle was a tribal elder and a powerful medicine man. Nali had to do what he was told.'

'I should think so. Disobeying a powerful medicine man isn't exactly a laughing matter,' Holt said. 'We have an ex-kadaicha man on Wungalla, although I don't believe he's completely shut up shop. I'll introduce you one day.'

'Oh, that would be *great!*' Riley regarded Holt McMaster with such a look of approval and respect. Marissa felt a momentary pang of ignoble jealousy. 'May I go find Georgia, sir?' he asked.

Marissa shook her head. 'You'll meet her soon, Riley.' She didn't want to curb his high spirits at the same time she thought they should take time to negotiate their way.

'Don't worry about him, he's fine,' Holt decided. 'She's out in the garden somewhere.'

Riley laughed happily. 'I really want us to be friends.'

Marissa forced herself to stay quiet. Making friends with a little person given to profligate tantrums might be easier said than done. On the other hand Riley could have a calming effect. His was the sunniest of natures when his short life had been full of troubles.

'Then off you go.' Holt McMaster gave him the okay. 'You've got plenty of space to play in. Don't go outside the compound wall?'

'Yes, sir!' Riley called, his small figure already flying down the steps.

'Right, I've got things to do,' Holt clipped off, 'but I won't say no to lunch. Make it 1:00 p.m., Olly. Meanwhile you can get Ms Devlin settled.'

'No problem,' Olly answered in the way that made Marissa feel very much at ease. So far so good. She thought she could even get used to Holt

McMaster's sardonic ways. 'Come on love. Follow me,' Olly said. 'Where's your luggage by the way?'

'Hal is bringing it in,' Holt turned back to remark. 'What there is of it. Marissa believes in travelling light.'

'Never mind, love,' Olly said comfortably. 'There's a really good store in Coorabri,' unknowingly echoing her boss's comment, 'where you'll be able to buy a few outfits for yourself and the boy. Beautiful child, I must say.'

Marissa prepared herself for yet another explanation of their relationship. Olly, like most people, probably assumed Riley was hers. 'He's as beautiful inside as out,' she said proudly.

'Let's hope some of it brushes off on Georgia,' Holt McMaster said before taking off down the steps.

He had all the grace of a natural born athlete, Marissa thought, looking after him. It was difficult *not* to. And something of a dancer thrown in. He was without question the most stunning looking man she had ever seen outside her own beloved father.

When she turned around, Olly's shrewd blue eyes were studying her. 'Come along now, love. Let's get you settled before lunch. You won't be meeting Mrs McMaster, Holt's grandmother, today but Georgia's aunt, Lois Aldridge, as I expect you know, will be back soon for lunch. You ride yourself?' Olly asked, not sounding terribly hopeful the answer would be in the affirmative.

'Yes, I do,' Marissa said, her eyes moving irresistibly all around the spacious entrance hall. The most transcendent feature was a very grand divided staircase with a huge stained-glass panel towering above the landing. The colours in the panel were simply wonderful! Graceful black wrought-iron balustrades encased the mahogany staircase. The floor was a traditional black and white marble. A circular library table stood on a circular Persian rug, centred beneath a huge crystal chandelier. The table displayed to advantage a stunning flower arrangement of masses of yellow roses, pine and dried twisted vines in a large Byzantine-gold container. There were paintings, as well. A console with a tall gilded mirror above it, two matching antique chairs with gilded bronze winged panthers supporting the arms, there just wasn't time to take everything in. Obviously this was a house of *serious* collectors.

'That's a blessing,' Olly was saying, sounding relieved. 'The last lass never could get the hang of it. One simply has to be able to ride on a station. What about young Riley?'

'He's a natural,' Marissa told her.

'Like mother, like son.'

Marissa *had* to make the relationship plain. 'He's my brother, Olly. Half brother really. He's my late father's.'

Olly swung about, clasping her hands together as though in prayer. 'Then where's his mother, child?'

'She's gone and she won't be coming back,' Marissa said, her voice matter-of-fact.

'Good Lord! This must be very hard for you, Marissa.' Olly paused, one hand on a newel. 'You're what, twenty-two, twenty-three?'

'Nearly twenty-four. It *is* hard, but I have a big consolation. I love Riley. He's my family.'

'Of course he is, love.' Without further comment Olly began to mount the staircase, taking the left hand side to the upper gallery also balustraded in the same decorative wrought-iron.

Whether Olly believed her was anyone's guess. With Riley constantly addressing her as *Ma,* it was becoming increasingly difficult to *be* believed. Yet she couldn't break him of the habit. Having a stable mother figure in his life loomed very large in Riley's mind.

The long corridors had polished floors with Persian runners absorbing their footsteps. The walls were showcases for portraits of the

McMaster ancestors, a handsome, rather arrogant looking lot like the present owner. Splendid looking chairs stood at intervals if one wanted to sit and admire them.

Olly paused as they came towards the end of the atmospheric hallway. 'The old schoolroom's in here, love.' She opened the door, inviting Marissa to enter.

'This has been here a while,' Marissa observed, gazing around the large room.

'Since the house was built.' Olly nodded. 'Quite a few little McMasters have studied here. Holt among them. Think you'll be happy here?'

Marissa smiled. 'Indeed I will! I'm very grateful for this job, Olly. It means I can have Riley with me I'm happy already!' The room was a little on the sombre side—nothing that couldn't be fixed with a touch of colour—but in perfect order. The walls were lined with bookcases filled with books, well thumbed for the most part, some even dog-eared. A large blackboard was set up near the windows. What looked like the original desks and chairs of some dark golden timber stood in neat rows, ten desks in all. Two marvellous globes on stands caught the eye, terrestrial, celestial.

'Does Georgia do her lessons here?' Marissa asked. If she did there was no sign of it.

'Miss Lois prefers to conduct the lessons down

in the Garden Room,' Olly said. Was that the merest trace of disapproval in her voice? 'If I might divulge a little secret—just between you and me—not many lessons are going on. I best warn you if Holt hasn't already done so, little Georgy is a bit of a handful.'

Marissa spoke without thinking. 'I would never have thought so with a father like that?'

'Meaning?' Olly's sparse eyebrows shot up.

'I can't imagine anyone with the temerity to step out of line.'

Olly laughed. 'Holt can cope with *anything* and does, but Georgy would break anyone's heart.'

'She wants her mother.' Marissa had great sympathy for the motherless little girl.

'She wants *a* mother,' Olly corrected. 'Tragically her mother didn't want *her.* Georgy is only little but she *knows* this. Abandonment is at the heart of her problems. You'll be the one to understand.'

'Oh, I do, Olly.' Marissa's blue eyes misted over. 'I'm hoping the children take to one another.'

'Don't expect results right away, love,' Olly warned. 'Come on now. I'll show you your rooms. They're across the hallway. Riley can have the room next to yours,' she said. 'If you like them, I'll have them aired and the beds made up.'

Both rooms had lovely views of the rear gardens,

though she realised all the rooms would have a view and wonder of wonders there was a fenced swimming pool. 'That's not a mirage is it?' Marissa asked, her eyes on the sparkling turquoise water. Swimming would build Riley up and help his condition. She was a good swimmer herself. She had made the University swim team. To the right of the pool was an open sided pool house with an orange terra cotta tiled roof. The stout pillars that supported the roof were wreathed in flowering morning glories. She could see sofas, tables, dining chairs, comfortable chaises. Great!

'Used all the time, love,' Olly told her casually. 'It's there to be enjoyed. You'll have plenty of time to yourself. Holt's father had it built for Holt and the girls.'

Marissa had to confront her lack of inside information. 'He has sisters? Forgive me, but I only met Mr McMaster today.'

'Seems he took a great liking to you,' Olly observed laconically.

'I wouldn't say that exactly—' Marissa shook her head, not believing he *had* '—but he did want to help us.'

'That's Holt.' Olly shrugged. 'He has two sisters, Alex—Alexandra—three years older married to *the* Steven Bailey, merchant banker turned politician, some say Prime Minister in waiting, and Francine, two years younger, a dedicated career woman, finance, not as yet married. Holt's father died in a tragic accident on the property not long after Holt was married. His mother remarried last year. She now lives in Melbourne, but she visits often.

'Holt's grandmother, Catherine, has never left Wungalla for any length of time since she came here as a bride. There have been many trips, of course. She has family in England but this is her home. She won't be parted from Holt or Wungalla. Holt is his mother's maiden name, by the way. He was christened Douglas Holt McMaster, but the Douglas never took. It was his uncle Carson, his mother's brother who started calling him Holt. He has the Holt dark eyes and that distinctive widow's peak. He must have told you he was divorced?' Olly looked Marissa right in the eye.

'He mentioned it briefly,' Marissa said. 'I can't believe my good fortune, Olly. These rooms have everything we could possibly want.'

Olly's expression softened. 'You don't have to dash down the hallway to get to the bathroom, either, love. Each bedroom and there are twelve have been fitted with an *en suite.*' She made a moue with her mouth as she said it. 'The rooms were big enough to allow for the renovations. If you want to make your surroundings a bit nicer there are things galore out in the storerooms. Such a lot of stuff overflowed from the house. I'm sure Holt won't mind if you pick out a few things. We aim to keep you happy.'

Marissa felt a knot in her throat. 'More than that I want to make everyone else happy,' she said. 'I love teaching. Riley picks up on everything so quickly.'

'Maybe Georgia can learn from that.' Olly's breath ended on a sigh.

'I expect Georgia knows how to swim?' Marissa took another peep at the glittering pool.

'Some hope!' Olly said. 'She *hates* the water.'

'That's hard to believe,' Marissa said, much surprised. 'I thought everyone loved the water. Riley is a great little swimmer for his age. Once Georgia sees him enjoying himself in the water she might feel differently.'

'Don't get your hopes up, love. Ah, this will be Hal with your luggage.' Olly went to the doorway, waving a hand.

Hal duly arrived, putting the two pieces of luggage down, then he turned and looked at Marissa. 'You haven't got much here have you, girlie?' He sweetened the remark with a smile.

Olly elbowed him hard in the ribs. 'No need for *you* to worry about that, Hal.'

'Only remarkin'.' Hal's voice took on an aggrieved note. 'You're such a tartar, Olly!'

Olly couldn't stop herself from giving him another hard nudge.

'Actually I have plenty of clothes, Hal,' Marissa said. 'Only they're in Brisbane where I come from.'

'You and the boy?' He gave her a sort of conspiratorial wink.

Marissa took it as yet another sign of misconception. 'Riley is my little brother.'

Hal flashed a quick look at Olly. 'Whatever you say, miss. You sure don't look like anyone's mother, a delicate creature like you. How come you talk so fancy?'

'Unlike *you,* Hal Brady, Marissa had a good education,' Olly said sternly. 'Now off you go. The garden calls.'

'Got my runnin' shoes on already.' Hal grinned. He sketched a quick salute, then made his exit.

'Real old woman is Hal,' Olly muttered, her face slightly heated. 'But he means well. Just to keep you goin', I've got a pile of Fran's things stored away. She doesn't wear them anymore. You'd be of a size. She's very slim, though she's taller than you, darn near six feet. All the McMasters are tall. I'll pull a few things out for you later on.'

Marissa felt touched but embarrassed. 'I *can* get through until Mr McMaster takes me shopping, Olly. He said he would.'

'Why let perfectly good things go to waste? Fran sure doesn't need 'em. She's a regular clothes horse. Besides, didn't you tell me you had to save up for young Riley's education?'

'Yes, I do.' Marissa moved to give Olly a spontaneous hug. 'Thank you for being so nice to me. It means a lot.'

Olly's narrow face blossomed with colour. 'That's okay, love. I reckon you need a little TLC. Well,' she said brightly, moving to the door, 'I'll leave you to settle in. Lunch at one. You might want to find young Riley before then. I haven't heard any screeches, I have to admit I was rather expecting a few, so the children must be getting on, or Riley can't find her. She has a hundred hiding places.'

'Don't worry, Olly.' Marissa went to the window, looking out. 'I'll go find them in a minute or two. Riley is an amazing little person. Georgia will find it hard to quarrel with him.'

Olly's gaze was sceptical. 'I hate to say it, but Georgy could quarrel with a stone. She's getting too much for me and I do my best, but Georgy is as wilfully moody as her mother.'

* * *

Left alone Marissa had a quick wash to freshen up. She changed her striped shirt for a nicer one, an embroidered T-shirt in the shade of red that suited her colouring so well. That done, she brushed out her hair, then took the time to put their things away. Some of the clothes needed ironing. Marj had let her use the washing machine and the dryer at the pub, but some things demanded ironing to look good.

She was very happy with their rooms. They were generously sized, both with queen-size beds and comfortable armchairs. Above her bed was a grouping of botanical prints in handsome gold frames; above Riley's a collection of prints of thoroughbreds. He would love those. It was accommodation any governess used to a shoe box and blank walls would die for.

She should have asked where Georgia's bedroom was but she would find out soon enough. From all accounts six-year-old Georgia was a real handful with all attempts at discipline washing off her like water. She had also learned Georgia had a mercurial personality like her mother. The mother who had abandoned her as Riley's mother had abandoned him. That was one big thing they would have in common, although Riley had come to terms with *his* mother's abandonment while

Georgia sounded like she was *furious* about it. Probably all the tantrums were a cry for attention. Holt McMaster might be doing his level best for her but he didn't particularly sound the doting dad. She disapproved of that. Georgia would need an awful lot of reassurance.

Time to go find them! Both children would need to wash their hands for lunch. She wondered what Aunt Lois would be like. A 'wilfully moody' woman like her sister? Marissa hoped not. It was good to know Riley would respect Holt's admonition not to go outside the home compound. Riley was an obedient child, a child of light.

Marissa had just reached the foot of the staircase when a young woman entered through the front door.

When she caught sight of Marissa she frowned heavily, looking Marissa up and down in hostile inquiry. 'Who are *you?*' There was a snap in her voice like a released elastic band.

Ah, another rambunctious one! 'I'm Marissa Devlin,' Marissa introduced herself as pleasantly as she could. 'Mr McMaster has hired me as the new governess.'

'He's *what?*'

It sounded as if Aunt Lois couldn't believe her ears. 'I'm Georgia's new governess,' Marissa repeated, her euphoric mood flattened in a second. 'And you would be Georgia's Aunt Lois?'

The haughty young woman held up a staying hand 'Just one moment. This is very difficult for me to take in. I had breakfast with Holt this very morning. He said *nothing whatsoever* about hiring a governess.'

Had he, Marissa had no doubt, Aunt Lois would immediately have talked him out of it. She was an attractive woman. It was her manner that wasn't. Her thick blond hair fell in a straight pageboy around a sharp featured but interesting face. She was wearing expensive riding clothes, cream silk shirt, fawn jodhpurs and burnished riding boots. She was fashionably bone thin, maybe a border-line anorexic.

Marissa hastened to placate this woman who was fairly sizzling with indignation. 'Mr McMaster wouldn't have known about me then. We met in Ransom. I was looking for work as a governess. He took me on.'

'What were you doing in Ransom? What are you doing out West anyway? What exactly are your qualifications? Who would know if you're to be believed or not? I just don't understand this.' Aunt Lois bit her lip. 'Georgia has been doing ex-tremely well under my tutelage.'

'I'm sure that's true—' Marissa kept up her valiant attempt at conciliation '—but Mr McMaster did say you had your own life in Sydney.'

Aunt Lois looked like she might go after Holt that very minute and kill him.

'If you *do* have qualifications, I would very much like to see them.'

'Mr McMaster has seen them,' Marissa told her, not at all intimidated by the other woman, though clearly she was meant to be. Even so, she was unhappy their meeting was going so badly.

Out in the driveway, the sound of a little girl yelling at the top of her voice cut through the golden stillness. It wasn't an angry yell or a frightened yell. To Marissa's trained ears, it sounded more like high excitement, fast getting out of control. Next came the sound of a dog barking. Marissa would know that bark anywhere. It was Dusty. Why wasn't he tied up? No way was Aunt Lois going to tolerate Dusty.

'What is going *on?*' Aunt Lois demanded in furious amazement. She turned to go back onto the verandah only a sandy headed little girl came flying up the steps with a mad urgency, followed by a worried looking Riley and an overexcited Dusty in full bound.

Aunt Lois screamed.

'Riley, Dusty!' Marissa tried for the voice of authority but couldn't get either's attention. Certainly not Georgia's. In fact she nearly got knocked down as the little girl—the heralded terror—tore into the entrance hall followed up by the extremely frisky Dusty, his tongue lolling, his strongly muscled body almost rigid with excitement, just loving the kids and the game.

Marissa was horrified, aghast at what damage might be done. Riley was trying desperately to control his beloved pet without a great deal of success. Her own commands were equally ineffectual. What a start! The odds were she would finish the day out of a job.

'Sit!' A man's voice cracked like a whip.

Dusty dropped on all fours, his expression previously so joyful, unmistakably shame faced. He knew he had done wrong.

Marissa thought *she* would be pleased to *sit,* too, her legs were so wobbly.

'He's a *lovely* dog, isn't he?' Georgia, who enjoyed nothing better than giving everyone a good fright, caught sight of her father and ran to him. 'His name is Dusty.'

Holt McMaster placed a restraining hand on her head. 'I've already had the pleasure of meeting Dusty, thank you, Georgy. Dusty is not, I repeat, *not* to come into the house. He can only come as far as the verandah. Have you got that, Riley?' He glanced at Riley who like Dusty was looking chastened.

'Yes, sir. I'm sorry he got so excited.' Ever gallant, Riley didn't add it was mainly because of Georgia's frenzied behaviour.

'*What* is going on here, Holt?' Aunt Lois, rubbing furiously at her temple, was looking at him in alarm. 'That ugly brute almost knocked me down.'

'Excuse *me,* he's *lovely!*' Georgia now full of truculence bellowed, a spindly little girl with a *big* voice. One foot kicked out in a temper, but mercifully didn't connect with anything.

'You're a wild, wild child, completely undisciplined!' Aunt Lois accused, on her own furious streak.

'Riley, take Dusty outside,' Marissa said quietly. 'How did he get here anyway?'

'Bart must have dropped him off.' Holt McMaster came up with the explanation.

One could scarcely expect a cattle baron used to hazards and even life threatening situations on a daily basis to take a small domestic incident too seriously.

'Take Dusty onto the verandah, Riley,' he instructed. 'I'll find you something to tie him up. Everything is okay now. You can relax.'

'Yes, sir.' Riley immediately brightened at Holt's level tone.

Georgia, the problem child, now walked up to Marissa *beaming* beatifically, displaying a missing front tooth. 'Are you Riley's mummy?' she asked as though absolutely thrilled at their arrival.

'*Wh-a-t?*' Aunt Lois's voice rose as shrill as a seagull's.

'Listen and learn, Lois,' Holt said.

Marissa went down to the little girl's level, smiling into the small freckled face. Georgia *was* plain at this stage. The missing tooth didn't help, but Marissa thought early adulthood would see a breakthrough. She certainly looked intelligent, even a character. Her fine wiry hair was sticking out at all angles as if electrified. It was sandy in colour with a tinge of orange, her eyes, her best feature, a clear light green. 'Hello, Georgy. I'm so pleased to meet you. I'm Marissa.' She offered her hand and the child took it with aplomb, as if trained from birth. 'I'm Riley's sister, not his mother. I'm here to help you with your lessons. Riley will be doing his with you. Would you like that?'

The beaming smile remained etched on Georgia's face. 'I'm thinking about it,' she said graciously as if it were all up to her. 'You're really, *really* pretty!' She suddenly inflated her cheeks to their full extent, then slowly released the air like a hissing balloon. 'Riley looks just like you. If you're not his Mummy why does he call you, Ma?' she asked, demonstrating she hadn't been behind the door when it came to intelligence. 'Why is he little and you're big?'

Aunt Lois cast her eyes heavenwards in scorn. 'Don't ask!'

Marissa had no choice but to ignore her. 'Ma is short for Marissa,' she explained to the child, though she knew too well it didn't sound like that when used by Riley. 'Riley was born a long time after I was. We have the same father, but different mothers.'

'Then where's his mother?' Georgia asked, engaging Marissa woman-to-woman. 'She should be here right *now*.' To emphasise the point she raised her small foot, encased in sturdy brown boots that went oddly with an expensive smocked dress, and stamped it hard on the marble floor.

'My father left Riley in *my* care, Georgia,' Marissa told her.

'No, call me Georgy!' the child said quickly. 'I like it. You've got a pretty voice, too.'

'Thank you.' Marissa smiled. 'Riley being with me works out well, Georgy. He's happy with me.'

'Because he *loves* you,' Georgia cried. It was a near operatic declaration. 'Can I go outside and talk to him?' She put out a hand fingering one of Marissa's silky, curls. 'Are these curls real? Just thought I'd check.'

Marissa nodded. 'Riley and I have naturally curly hair.'

'And it looks *great* on you! I really *loathe* my hair.' Georgia sighed deeply.

'Actually, Georgy, all your hair needs is the right preparation for flyaway hair.' Marissa wisely decided on the truth. 'You have so much life in you, it gets into your hair. All you do is rub the dressing between your palms, then smooth it over your hair. You'll find it works. One needs things to keep curly hair under control.'

'So that's it then!' Georgia sounded like she had been waiting years for a solution. 'Can we get some?' Abruptly she spun about, the steam of in-dignation coming off her. 'Why didn't *you* get me some?' she demanded of her aunt, bridling like a grown woman.

'All your hair needs is a good *brush,*' Aunt Lois insisted, looking like she wanted to give her niece a good whack with the said brush. 'That's if you'd stand still long enough.'

Holt McMaster appeared to Marissa's eyes, to be bored to distraction. Wearily he cut in. 'Now we've got *that* settled, maybe we can move on.'

'Just a sec, Holt.' Georgia flashed him an engaging smile, turning back to Marissa. 'Maybe we can try a new style?' Her sandy eyebrows arched in enquiry.

'Your hair doesn't *need* styling,' Aunt Lois exploded, foolish enough to break in again when anyone else would have left well alone. Only Lois was enormously put out her wretched little niece had taken a liking to the single mother Holt had brought into his home.

'Who asked *you?*' Georgia shouted rudely. 'I'm talking to Marissa, okay?'

'Holt, are you going to allow her to talk to me like that?' Lois pleaded.

'Sorry, I must have nodded off,' he groaned. 'That's quite enough, Georgy. Apologise to your aunt.'

'Don't worry, Holt, I *will.*' Georgia who really was being naughty, launched into a spirited little tap dance. '*Sorry,* Auntie!' She said, stopping her tap dance abruptly, arms outstretched.

'Oh, for goodness' sake, give us a break, Georgy,' Holt groaned. 'It seems to me, you could make quite a good living as a child movie star. You can go outside and join Riley for as long as it takes to tie Dusty up. After that, the two of you can wash your hands for lunch.'

'Thank you very much, *sir.*' Georgia smiled up at him sweetly, or as sweetly as her missing tooth would allow, having very smartly picked up on Riley's form of address for her father.

Marissa laughed, despite herself. The child was an entertainer in the making.

'Don't encourage her,' Aunt Lois ordered stiffly, giving Marissa a green glare.

'I'm sorry,' Marissa apologised. She knew she shouldn't have laughed, but Georgia definitely had a comedic flair.

'It really won't do to encourage her,' Aunt Lois repeated, pink flags of colour in her cheeks.

'You've made your point, Lois,' Holt McMaster said, mildly, watching Georgia run out on to the verandah where she favoured Riley, who was sitting on the steps, with a womanly pat on the cheek. Maybe Riley would replace Zoltan, who was always getting her to do the wrong thing.

'I suppose you're not telling the truth about yourself and the boy?' Lois turned on Marissa quite bitterly for someone she'd only just met.

'Why would I *not* be?' Marissa countered, trying to hide her upset. She hadn't realised there could be someone even more awful than her aunt Allison.

Lois gave her a sarcastic stare. 'Even a six-year-old child isn't buying your story.'

Holt called for a ceasefire. 'Marissa doesn't have to listen to that, Lois,' he said, his expression full of a deep impatience 'Apart from anything else, it's none of your business.'

Lois squeezed anguished hands together. 'After all I've done?' she cried, wild eyed. 'Hardly a day goes by without Georgia punching, kicking, screaming, *swearing,* and I'm the only who cares.'

Holt kept a tight rein on his temper. 'That's simply not true and you know it. Your help has been very much appreciated, Lois. I'm sure I've told you that many times, but you must be desperate for a break from Georgy?'

Marissa didn't need any little bird to tell her Aunt Lois would endure a dozen little savages who punched, kicked and swore like a wharfie just to be near him. And now she looked like she was getting dumped? So much for appreciation! Holt McMaster was one tough hombre. Marissa understood all at once she had been hired so Aunt Lois would no longer have a good reason to stay. He had *faked* that kindness.

The reason behind Marissa's sudden employment must also have occurred to Lois judging from the look on her face. 'Holt, what are you saying?' She spoke in a low rush, looking up at him. To her he was the most wonderful man in the *entire* world, but he had said something exceptionally brutal.

Time to make my getaway, Marissa thought, beset by cynicism.

'Would you excuse me,' she said. 'I have a spare lead for Dusty. I'll get it.' She couldn't bear to listen to the rest of this pleading, especially with Holt McMaster looking like he had no feelings at all. She hadn't taken to Aunt Lois one teeny bit given Aunt Lois had only wanted to attack her, but she had to admit to feeling a little sorry for the woman. It must be hell being in love with your sister's ex-husband. Probably she had been in love with him when she was chief bridesmaid at their wedding. She must have thought then, end of story, only the marriage hadn't worked out. A never to be missed opportunity had presented itself and Aunt Lois had seized it.

While not unsympathetic, Marissa couldn't help thinking Aunt Lois didn't stand a chance.

CHAPTER FOUR

IT TOOK Georgia less than twenty-four hours to decide she didn't want to remain in her own bedroom. She wanted to join Club Devlin in the west wing. Used to pushing and pushing for whatever she wanted, she was starting to sound a bit strident, repeating herself over and over.

'I want to come over to you, please, please, Marissa! We shouldn't be all over the place. We should be together!'

Riley ran his fingers anxiously through his curls wondering what having Georgia over might mean. He had never met such an explosive kid in his life.

'God, you're a dreadful child!' Lois stood at the door of the schoolroom, listening in. She felt vindicated at hearing her niece playing up on the unwanted governess.

Marissa was going about arranging the classroom the way she wanted it, while the children sat at their desks drawing whatever they fancied. In

Riley's case an excellent representation of a space shuttle complete with astronaut in his space gear; in Georgia's, a forest of gnarled trees standing in some kind of swamp inhabited by fierce four legged black creatures that Riley identified as wild boar.

At the sound of Lois's cutting voice the chatter stopped. 'What would *you* know?' Georgia swung into stride, screeching over her shoulder.

Really she was being baited Marissa thought, but took the time to correct the child. 'Georgia, please turn around and go on with your drawing,' she said, slipping easily into her schoolteacher mode. It had proved effective in the past, though her girls had never behaved remotely as badly as Georgia. 'If you expect to have your wishes con-sidered, you must act in a courteous manner. It's not nice to shout at your aunt.'

'Okay, sorry,' Georgia said gruffly, adding a par-ticularly ugly boar to her drawing. 'Tell *her* to quit being rude and shouting at me. You haven't heard her. Neither has Holt.'

'Shouldn't you call your father, *Daddy?*' Riley couldn't understand how Georgia came to be using her father's first name.

Georgia turned fully to face him. 'He doesn't mind, Riley,' she assured him. 'He likes it.'

Riley didn't look convinced. 'I always called my father Daddy.'

'Okay, I'll call Holt Daddy, if it'll please you!' Georgia had no wish to put Riley offside. She was absolutely enchanted with him. In fact he was so much fun he'd put Zoltan out of her head. 'I really love him. He's a great guy. I just wish I was a boy like you, then he'd love me more. Why are boys so bloody important?' She threw off the swear word effortlessly, demonstrating it was one of her favourites.

Marissa shook her head. 'No swearing, Georgy.'

Georgia's face settled into a wicked grin. 'Can I say damn and blast?'

'Only if you *really* have to say it,' Marissa said. 'As in falling over and hurting yourself, but I prefer you didn't. We're going to be learning lots and lots of new words. We won't need swear words, I promise.'

'It's *true,* Georgy,' Riley said, taking another look at her *wild* drawing. It made his look *ordinary.* She had added what looked like a clump of black barbed wire. 'I love words.'

'So do I,' Georgia said earnestly. 'But I love swearing, too,' she whispered behind her hand. 'I won't swear at you and Marissa. You're too nice.'

'Could I see you outside, Ms Devlin?' Lois asked

very shortly indeed, her eyes dark with multiple re-sentments and thwarted hopes.

'Of course.' Marissa paused for a moment to speak to the children. 'When you finish your drawing, Georgy, would you like to show Riley your favour-ite books and Riley can show you his. There's a big selection in the bookcases. I'll be right outside.'

'So, can I shift my bedroom down to you guys?' Georgia called after her, a lot of appeal in her hoarse little voice.

'We'll talk to your father about that,' Marissa said. 'I can't see he'll have any objection, but we must ask.'

'You're not going to see him today unless you go looking for him,' Georgia warned her. 'You can find him.' She turned about to offer encourage-ment. 'I know where he is. I'll tell you. Riley and I can find plenty of things to do, can't we, Riley?'

'You bet!' Riley laughed, a carefree sound that was music to Marissa's ears. 'This is a marvel-lous place.'

'We'll see.' Marissa kept walking to the door, wondering if it might be a good idea to find Holt McMaster and settle the matter. Georgia wouldn't give up. 'Rome wasn't built in a day,' she remarked. 'Please remember, Riley, the two of you must stay inside the home compound at all times.'

'Right, Ma!' Riley promised.

As she went out the door she heard Riley launch into a thumbnail sketch of Julius Caesar, undisputed master of ancient Rome and how he came to his gory end. Georgia hung on his every word.

Lois beckoned Marissa farther down the corridor, her face tight and cold. 'You're really going all out to ingratiate yourself here, aren't you? Holt, Olly, even my quite impossible little niece. I suppose you'll drop a curtsy to Mrs McMaster, when you meet her?'

Breathe in. Breathe out. Count to ten. Maybe fifteen. 'Why do you dislike me so much, Ms Aldridge?' she asked, wishing it weren't so. 'You don't even know me. I don't want to be on bad terms with you, rather the reverse. What's the problem? Georgy does need a governess and a firm hand. I'm hoping to supply both.'

The reasonable approach didn't touch Lois. The unwelcome glare never left her eyes. She didn't want conciliation. She wanted confrontation. 'I suppose because you've had a child you think you know all about how to handle them?' There was a bitter twist to her mouth. She was nearing thirty and her biological clock was ticking away like a time bomb. It was all *too* sad!

'Why in the world do I have to keep repeating

myself.' Marissa gave a heartfelt sigh. 'Riley is my half brother. I don't seem to be able to get you to understand that.'

Lois made an unladylike snorting sound. 'Stupid to deny it,' she spoke scornfully. 'It can be easily checked out.'

'Maybe then I can expect an apology?'

Lois didn't answer.

'What is it you wish to see me about?' Marissa asked, not wanting to hang around crossing swords.

'I actually want to *warn* you,' Lois said, her eyes glowing eerily. 'My sister may have left Georgia in Holt's care, but she is *still* Georgia's mother and she's *still* in love with Holt no matter what she says. Don't try to get too close to him, that's all.'

Marissa suddenly felt intensely irritated. 'I have no intention whatever of getting *too close* to him, Ms Aldridge, whatever that means. Maybe you can relay that to your sister. I'm sure you report to her.'

'Why ever not!' Colour flew into Lois's cheeks. 'She *is* my sister.'

And I bet she knows you're in love with him. Probably gets a cruel kick out of it.

'What?' The word came out like a gunshot. Lois obviously had ESP. She had read Marissa's mind.

'I didn't say anything,' Marissa protested.

'What can you possibly get out of burying yourself way out here?' Lois changed tack. 'I have noticed how pretty you are.' She couldn't bring herself to say lovely.

'I need to keep Riley with me until he's old enough to go to school,' Marissa made another bid for understanding. 'It proved too difficult in the city. A good friend of mine was raised on the land. She had a governess. She was the one who suggested I try governessing for a year or two. Riley was devastated when our father died. He needs me close by for a while.'

'So you're going to persist with your story?' Lois asked, her nostrils pinched. This was all a bad dream—a nightmare really—this girl coming here. Lois could see Trouble written all over her.

'No story, Ms Aldridge, it's true.' Marissa was quite aware of Lois's silent fears. They shocked her. 'I must go back to the children.'

'You don't appear to be doing a good job so far,' Lois snapped in satisfaction.

'Actually things are going a lot better than I anticipated. I'm immensely grateful. Do please excuse me.'

But Lois was in a foul temper, an unfortunate trait that appeared to run in the family. 'I suggest you don't go after Holt. Georgia has a beautiful room of her own. *I* was the one who refurbished it. Leave well alone.'

Please, God, help! Marissa stopped, then turned around. 'I'm sure you've been a very good aunt to Georgia, Ms Aldridge, but I answer to Mr McMaster. He *is* my employer.' She had to stand her ground, even in the light of Lois's aggression. 'I may have needed the job, but I would never have taken it if I wasn't going to have a free hand.'

'Free hand!' Lois gave her a furious look. 'Okay, have it your own way! But make an enemy of me and my sister and you'll be sorry.'

That sounded like a *threat.* Marissa retraced her steps so she was standing only a foot away from Lois. 'I wonder if you're not overestimating your own power?' she asked quietly, dismayed at inciting so much dislike. She could have pointed out Holt McMaster had already told Lois not to interfere, but she simply didn't have the heart. Everything about Lois screamed here was a woman tearing herself to pieces over a forbidden man. Marissa wasn't even sure if one could marry one's sister's ex-husband? Probably. Lots of things had changed.

Lois's cheeks went from pink to crimson. 'You're certainly different from the other governesses we've had.' Her voice shook with outrage.

'How dare you speak to me like that. I'm *family*.
You're an employee. And not for long, I can assure
you of that. I'm a tabby cat compared to my sister.
She's a tigress.'

Marissa didn't doubt that for a moment. Holt
McMaster wouldn't have married a tabby cat. 'Is
that why she didn't like the desert?' she asked,
before going on her way.

Marissa sought Olly's advice before leaving the
house. She found her in the kitchen, writing up
menus.

'Georgy wants to change bedrooms,' she said,
coming right to the point. 'She wants to shift down
to our wing. She appears to have taken a great
fancy to Riley, praise the Lord!'

'I'm not surprised,' Olly said. 'Take a seat. He's
a beautiful sunny-natured child, a great credit to
you, Marissa.'

'Thank you.' Marissa felt besieged by mistaken
assumptions, even from Olly. 'What do *you*
think?' She slipped into a chair, studying Olly's
slightly worried expression.

'Lois put a lot of money and time into refurbish-
ing Georgy's bedroom,' Olly pointed out, looking
at Marissa over the top of her glasses. 'Very ex-
travagant and much too grown-up for a little girl,

if you ask me, but of course she didn't. I don't think she knows any other way. Tara was the same.'

'Tara being the ex-Mrs McMaster?'

'One and the same,' Olly said, brushing away a bothersome insect. 'It makes sense the child wanting to be near you. Certainly you can keep a better eye on her. She hasn't for a while, but she used to sleepwalk.'

Sleepwalk? Marissa found herself drooping a bit. 'Oh, that must have been a worry?' She waited for Olly to say more.

'It *was,* but that phase seems to be over.'

'Thank God for that, but she would still need watching. I was planning on asking Mr McMaster for his permission, but I wanted to consult you first. If you don't think it's a good idea I won't go ahead. Ms Aldridge—I haven't been invited to call her Lois—'

'And I don't think you ever will be,' Olly cut in, dryly.

Marissa nodded her agreement. 'Ms Aldridge is very much against the idea.'

'Well, she would be, wouldn't she, love? By the way, in case you've missed it, Miss Lois is very *fond* of Holt.'

'I have gathered that along the way,' Marissa said, without expression. 'She told me—warned me might be closer—not to do anything that would upset her sister.'

Olly made a clicking sound with her tongue. 'Tara is the dominant one of the two,' she confided. 'Lois is a pale shadow of her older sister. In fact I don't think I'd be exaggerating in saying she goes in awe of Tara, though she's nearly thirty years old.'

Marissa propped her chin on her hand. 'That's sad. I did, however, receive a clear message. If I did anything to anger Georgy's mother I'd be out of here like a shot.'

'Hey, now!' Olly moved her head closer to Marissa's. 'The ex-Mrs McMaster carries no clout around here, love. Don't let Lois fool you. She wouldn't be so angry if you were on the plain side. But let's face it, love, you're *not!* That's what's putting her nose out of joint. You turn up here, out of nowhere, looking like the Rose of Tralee. I suppose it's natural for Lois to feel threatened.'

Marissa gave a moan of dismay. 'Oh, Olly, I'm here as Georgy's governess. That's the only way I should be regarded. I'm no threat to anyone, I assure you. I've got quite enough on my plate.'

'Sure you have!' Olly agreed. 'But there's no denying beauty wields a lot of power. Besides, the fact you've got so much on your plate, is exactly why a rich husband wouldn't go astray.'

'I'm not even tempted, Olly,' Marissa said, aghast at what Olly might be implying.

'Righto!' Olly answered.

'The last governess fell in love with Mr McMaster, didn't she?'

'And the one before that! Both of them, head over heels. Holt is in no hurry to remarry—who could blame him—but he could have his pick of a dozen eligible young women this very day. And those are just the ones I know about.'

Probably the rest could form a queue to Alice Springs. 'How did he meet Tara?' Marissa dared to ask. 'Are the Aldridges a landed family?'

Olly shook a head covered in short, soft grey curls. 'Things might have worked out if they were. No, Holt met Tara at some big society party in Sydney, where the family live. The father is a prominent businessman. He always makes The Rich List anyway. The wedding was *huge!* By the time Holt got back from the honeymoon in Europe I think he was having second thoughts.'

'Lordy!' Marissa exclaimed. Might it not then be a good idea to have a trial run? 'He doesn't seem the sort of man to make mistakes?' And having made one, live comfortably with it.

'We *all* make mistakes, love.' Olly reached over and patted Marissa's hand consolingly.

She had a long way to go before she could convince anyone Riley wasn't her love child.

The utility rattled across the open plains that ran out to the horizons, flat as a board. No wonder the countryside was inundated in times of flood, Marissa thought. She drove with her arm out of the window, enjoying the breeze and the amazing spectacle of thousands of birds taking flight as the ute approached; the many coloured mulga parrots, the cheeky white cockatoos, big pale grey galahs with their purplish-pink breasts and to her intense delight one of the great sights of the Outback she had heard about, the massed squadrons of budgerigar on manoeuvres. She watched in fascination as they wheeled, twisted, turned in perfectly coordinated formation. Over the years she had seen caged budgies of many different and often exquisite colours, but in the wild they had only one colour form: green with fine dark stripes across the head and back with a bright yellow face. She could even see blue bands on the top of the bills. How absolutely lovely all these wonderful birds! Not in small numbers but thousands upon thousands. The Outback, especially the Channel Country she was finding was swarming with a rich and hugely varied bird life.

One thing to admire the V formations in the sky, another to avoid trouble on the ground. 'Oh, my gosh!' She braked hard, her heart jumping into her mouth. A group of wallabies reared up out of a patch of long golden grass, startling her as much as the sound of the utility had startled them. They stared at her with mild curiosity but no sign of alarm when she could have ploughed into them, then losing interest, bounded away towards the silver glitter of water.

She drove on, deciding safety lay in keeping her eyes in what lay in front of her, no matter what magnificent birds took to the air. Those dusty 4WDs were fitted with bull bars for a good reason. According to directions from Georgy and Olly, essentially the same, she was to follow the course of a long shallow billabong overhung with great River Red Gums. It meandered away to her right where the wallabies had headed. She drove in closer until she could see the labyrinth of roots they were sending out towards the water.

What she had to look for was clouds of red dust that would mark the holding yard where the men were working that day. She drove steadily, revelling in the peace and freedom. To her city eyes, the sweeping landscape looked wild and untamed. She had no difficulty understanding how appallingly easy it would be to get lost, dreadful prospect! Not that far off, billows of red dust began spiralling in great puffs into the amazingly blue sky. She felt quite pleased with herself, finding the camp so easily, when she had never prided herself on her sense of direction. It was great to have her own vehicle to transport herself. Holt had promised her she wouldn't be tied to the homestead or the home compound like the children. She couldn't wait to explore.

It was certainly very hot but she wasn't finding it hard to bear. The high humidity of the tropics was worse she thought. There was no guarantee Holt would say yes to Georgia's wish to change bedrooms, but she had to try for the child. She had been expecting a difficult settling in period, but Riley's presence had worked like a charm. Despite predictions to the contrary the children had joined forces. That filled her with gratitude.

The closeness of the spiralling dust cloud was an illusion she found. The holding yard was farther off than she thought. She accelerated towards her destination, noticing the banks of the billabong, at this stretch more a chain of rocky gullies, were rising more steeply. The scrub, too, was becoming denser, the giant river gums spreading their canopies over the water. Now she could hear noises carrying on the wind; lowing cattle, dogs barking, the crack of whips. In mustering time she supposed the place would be alive with men on horseback and motorbikes, choppers whirring overhead.

A movement in a patch of chest high yellow grass attracted her attention. The bright red track was badly rutted in places, slowing her down. More wallabies? A full grown kangaroo? A dingo, camouflaged by the scorched grasses the same colour as its coat, a wild pig? A few tremors moved through her. What did she know about the vast Inland? Absolutely nothing. It could hold terrors she had never even thought of. The *shape* was moving stealthily. Every movement further disturbed its cover. She prayed it would be a lone wallaby. A kangaroo would have to be too tall, so would an emu.

In the next instant, almost turning her to stone, a fearsome dragon, dark brown, almost black, strikingly marked with yellow spots lumbered out onto the track, turning its head towards her.

For God's sake! She braked right away. It had to be a perentie, surely the biggest one around. King of all lizards, it was at least seven feet long and if that weren't frightening enough, it was emitting a fierce hiss along its extended neck pouch and out of its fork tongued mouth. She had read these lizards could be aggressive. She'd never seen one bigger than a frilled neck or a blue tongue in her entire life. She couldn't risk provoking it. She brought the ute to a halt, more than happy to give the beast right of way. She was even prepared to sit there half the day if needs be, until this relic from prehistoric times thundered across the track.

There was a whole wilderness for it to run around in. Why squat there staring balefully at her? Was it possible it was protecting a nearby nest? They were close to water. She knew these huge goannas could swim. Its powerful tail was swishing from side to side, giving her the dismal impression it was about ready to lash out. Should she take off like a bat out of hell? Surely the ute could outrun a perentie? Her hands on the wheel shook as the dragon like creature suddenly reared up on its back legs— something she didn't even know it *could* do—surveying her like a victim at its mercy. To her horror, it was standing as tall as a man.

Go away, please, she begged silently.

The creature didn't back off an inch.

She couldn't afford to sit there waiting for it to charge her and maybe bound onto the hood? A crocodile could scarcely have intimidated her more. Where was her backbone? She was showing her inexperience. Marissa thumped the wheel, then took off, jaw locked, nerves popping with strain, taking a sharp right and accelerating away towards the line of gullies. She almost expected the perentie to be flying alongside like something out of Prehistoric Park. She was sure she had read somewhere they had an amazing turn of speed.

Off the beaten track the going was really rough. She had to hold tight to the wheel, risking quick looks in the rear vision. *Nothing.* She must have worn it down. There was no dinosaur galloping after her, but she was bouncing around in her seat like a clown in a pantomime.

A mile off Holt lifted his head at the sound of a speeding vehicle. He had been intending to drive to another site instead he reached into the Jeep for his binoculars, training them over the landscape. One sweep and he caught a red ute in a screen of dust. It was swerving all over the place. Then it straightened out, heading straight for the chain of gullies.

What the hell was going on? Anxiety not unmixed with anger flared. This was rough country. Why hadn't she kept to the track? Surely she wasn't just fooling around? One thing was certain: She was driving much too fast. She had him worried. He threw the binoculars onto the backseat, then with undisguised irritation jumped behind the wheel, slewing the Jeep around and driving off in the direction of the speeding utility. It was fast disappearing into the thicket of scrub.

He had an awful vision of her crashing into branches; careening down the slope; overturning the ute in the rocky bed of a gully. She had never been Outback in her life. She didn't look as though butter would melt in her mouth, yet there she was hooning around rugged country churning up dust. Anything for a bit of excitement! He should never have given her permission to leave the compound on her own. He was angry with himself for trusting her. And just what was supposed to be happening to the children while she was out on her little jaunt?

Silly fool! he muttered furiously. He would have thought she had far too much sense.

He found her sitting forlornly in the ute, its front wheels bogged in the churned up mud. Once he saw she was okay he felt not one twinge of pity.

'Are you going to tell me what the hell you thought you were doing?' he asked on a soft rasp. 'You might as well get out of there. The ute's not going anywhere in a hurry.' He opened the door, extending an impatient hand.

She took it.

Her skin was as soft as the petals of a rose, yet there was that sizzle again at the slightest brush of skin. She was clinging to his hand tightly until she was able to steady herself, two feet on the creek bed. He could feel her shaking. Obviously she had given herself a good chastening fright. Abruptly his anger abated. 'Did you hurt yourself anywhere?' He let his eyes move over her; past the silky masses of curls, so very feminine, that haloed her lovely, dreamy face, down over the delicate, long legged body any man would approve. He had never met a girl—a woman—like this in his whole lifetime. Not one he had an irresistible urge to touch.

Get a grip, man!

She was shaking her head. 'I'm sorry.' She spoke in a suitably subdued voice, turning up her head to stare at him with enormous blue eyes.

'So you should be,' he bit off, determined to subdue the pounding in his blood. 'From now on you're under surveillance. It could have been a whole lot worse. You could have rolled the ute.'

'I know.' She was repentant. Water lapped her ankles, soaking her shoes and the hem of her trousers but she didn't even notice it. The way she felt the water could have been steaming *hot!*

'Nobody should be that stupid,' he muttered disapprovingly, making a real effort to shake off the effect she was having on him. A woman used her fragility to bring out a man's protective streak, he thought, stunned by his own susceptibility. Of course it had to happen some time, but this was Georgy's governess, for God's sake!

'I know. I know.' To Marissa's horror her legs suddenly gave way from under her.

'Aw, hell!' He reacted swiftly, getting a tight supporting arm around her. It brought her right up against his body, all but shattering his composure. Even for a man like him, a man who had trained himself to resist temptation, it sent out shock waves. 'It's all right. I've got you!' She was all but in his arms.

Marissa was too breathless to reply. Her body felt engulfed by heat. She was one quivering mass of sensation. The terror was, she was betraying that agitation. She wasn't a complete innocent, inexperienced around men, yet this man's touch turned her muscles to jelly.

'I'm sorry,' she gasped out an excuse. 'I must be in shock.'

'Could be.' He crouched a little to hoist her into his arms, while she made a helpless gesture with her hands. 'Just relax.' He strode across the rocky bed of the gully and up onto the sandy bank.

'It's okay now,' she protested, marvelling how her body fitted so neatly to his. 'You can put me down.' Those powerful arms that enclosed her weren't offering comfort. Rather she felt a hard impatience in him that helped sober her up. As it was, her heart was beating like a large bird penned in a tiny cage.

'I should think so. You weigh a ton!' he groaned, as he lowered her to the pale ochre sands.

'I *don't!*' Her answer was an automatic wail.

'Oh, what does it matter? We'll sit for a minute.' He sounded mightily annoyed. He was, but Marissa didn't know the real reason.

She was getting to him. Plain and simple. Far from weighing a ton she had felt incredibly soft and fragile in his arms. Her skin gave off a light ellusive fragrance he found very seductive. He almost wished he didn't care about hurting her. But he did. This young woman had been caught up in enough trouble. Time to do something to defuse the situation.

'Do you know how stupid that was leaving the track and speeding through stretches of long grass?' he asked, crisply, folding his long length on the sand. 'You could have struck a rock or a huge rut or some animal perfectly camouflaged by the grass. You don't have a roo bar on the ute. You'll have to get one.'

She risked a sideways glance at his strong, handsome profile. Right then it was more than a little *brooding*. 'It was a goanna.' She knew it was time to explain herself, regain some respect. 'A perentie, isn't it? It had to be seven or eight feet long and it *stood up.*' Her voice still held traces of shock. 'I had no idea they could do that. It lumbered out of the grass and planted itself on the track right in front of me. I don't believe a crocodile could have frightened me more.'

He laughed in an abrupt change of mood. 'How close have you been to a crocodile?' He didn't even try to keep the mockery out of his voice.

'As close as I want to be.' She couldn't control an involuntary shudder. 'I've seen them on wild life shows. They're pretty fearsome creatures.'

'And amazing! They've outlived the dinosaurs. I've flown a helicopter extensively through the Territory so I've seen hundreds in swamps, lakes, rivers. If you'd seen a croc up close you'd think a perentie could be trained as a pet. Did you think of beeping the horn? Stupid question!'

She rallied at his look of scorn. 'I *didn't* for the simple reason I was terrified of doing anything to provoke it. It looked like it was going to charge the ute and clamber up onto the hood. I know they can climb trees.'

His glittering eyes narrowed sharply over her. 'I suppose it's just possible it was protecting a nest.'

'That fact had occurred to me,' she said tartly, suddenly reckless.

'So you weren't hooning around after all. You were taking evasive action.' He laughed again. 'I promise I won't tell anyone about this.'

'I wish I could be sure about that.'

His eyes came back to hold hers. 'Didn't you hear the word *promise?*'

Lord but this man made her feel vulnerable. And, what was a great deal more dangerous, very much a woman. If she was going to stay on as Georgia's governess she would have to learn how to handle it. 'I was scared it was going to come after me. Don't laugh. I hit a deep rut and lost control of the wheel for a minute or two. By the time I managed to get it back again, the ute was hurtling towards the gully with a mind of its own. The mud locked around the wheels like cement.'

'Well, you were lucky,' he said. 'I suppose the real question is, what are you *doing* out here?'

He couldn't help himself. His gaze was drawn to her mouth, so soft and cushiony, beautifully shaped A mouth for kissing.

It made Marissa so nervous she slid the tip of her tongue around her lips to moisten them.

Holt almost let out a sigh. She should be very grateful he was such a gentleman. 'I thought I hired you as the governess, teaching the children their lessons, supervising their play, stuff like that?'

Her white skin flushed. 'Olly is looking in on them while I'm away. I've given them things to do. I drove out here because Georgy wants to shift out of her bedroom and join us in the west wing.'

'Is that a fact?' He might have sounded teasing, but inside he felt pretty heated. Did she know everything about her was charming him?

'Well…yes.'

'And you drove all the way out here to ask me if it's okay?'

'Was there someone *else* I should ask?'

'Now, now, Ms Devlin!' His clipped tones became a deep taunting, 'Don't totally forget yourself. The idea is to act respectful.'

Of course it was! She picked up a pebble and hurled it at the water, finding some satisfaction in seeing it bounce several times across the surface. 'Believe me I'm *trying*. You're Georgy's father. The person I should consult. Her aunt Lois is very much against it.'

'Well, that's par for the course!' He fell back on his elbow, his long, lean body faultlessly arranged. 'All that money and imagination squandered! I suppose Georgy lost no time making her demands?'

Marissa shrugged her shoulders, *amazed* she was sitting on the banks of an Outback billabong with one of the nation's cattle barons resting nonchalantly beside her, even if he was making infuriating little comments. 'She's set on it, but it's not really a bad idea. I can keep a better eye on her and you may have noticed she's taken a great liking to Riley.'

'And you,' he said, 'for which I'm immensely relieved. Out of nowhere, on the face of it, the answer to my fervent prayers! Are you feeling any better?'

What kind of answer could she give? That she was feeling *excited,* nearly breathless as if something extraordinary was about to happen. There was such a charge in the air. It was dangerously worrying. Things seemed to be moving very fast. She slicked a stray curl away from her cheek. 'I'm fine,' she announced which wasn't strictly true. 'Right now I'm worried about the ute.'

'Don't be,' he said, slamming a door on his own unruly thoughts. 'We'll get it out of there for you. Meanwhile I'd best get you back to your duties.' He stood up in one lithe movement, holding out a hand to her.

Panic shot through her at the thought of renewed contact.

How stupid am I?

But he released her quickly.

She gave herself another moment to be sure her voice wouldn't betray her. 'Thank you for rescuing me,' she said, 'although I think I could have walked to your camp.'

He frowned. 'I'd prefer you not to do that when I'm not around.' It was definitely an order, even if it was fairly gently couched.

'Whatever you say.' As they walked up the grassy slope, she began to laugh softly. 'Did you *really* think I was acting wildly?' She mightn't be the best driver in the world but she was careful, considerate, not given to manic bursts.

'I have to say I was surprised,' he admitted, further seduced by the sound of her laughter.

'And Georgy? I have the go-ahead?'

'To do what?' He stopped abruptly, staring down at her. She *had* to know how desirable she was, the effect she had on men.

The hard note in his voice utterly confused her. His eyes were as black as night, brilliant but fathomless. It was one of those moments that seemed to go on forever. 'Why, shift her things to the west wing!' she explained. Every nerve in her body felt wired.

He nodded curtly and walked on. 'If that's what she wants.'

'You love your daughter?'

He broke his stride. 'Excuse me, Ms Devlin? You ask me *that* and think you can get away with it?'

Had she cast off all common sense like a rope? 'Forgive me,' she apologised, 'of course you do. It's just…sometimes you sound a little remote.'

'You've really been studying me, haven't you?' he asked.

Why was that strange? He had been studying her.

'I like to get a picture of people,' she said.

'So do I. To help you out, I'm tough on the *outside,* Ms Devlin. Any other questions?'

She was quiet for a moment. 'Do you mind if I do something to brighten up the schoolroom?' She was jogging now just to keep up with him. He had work to do. He wanted to be rid of her.

'What do you have in mind, posters, billowing sails, bunting?'

'What about a lick of paint?' she countered. 'It wouldn't cost you too much.'

Her little show of bravado dissolved as he turned to face her, so tall she felt pint-sized when she wasn't. 'Just see *you* don't,' he said, sounding dead set serious.

'I beg your pardon?' She could feel herself flush.

'Don't *you* cost me any trouble,' he said.

For a moment she felt as though her mind had

seized up. 'I hardly know what you mean.' Not true. She knew they had connected day one.

He shook his head. 'I think you do.'

She deemed it best to remain silent. Better silent than try to grapple with the fact they had made that connection. Made it on sight. It really did *cloud* things when she needed everything to be perfectly clear.

How many men has she slept with? Holt thought as he drove her back to the homestead. *How many have touched her flawless white skin with insolent hands, intent on their own pleasure. Who was the man or boy who had seduced her?*

He felt an impotent anger that shocked him. It wasn't often he was disturbed by his own behaviour, but he was now. He had to question exactly why he had hired her, sympathy for her situation, liking for the boy? Or was it because of the beauty of her, the *unexpectedness* of her, like a white rose growing on a sand dune. Already she had alienated Lois who was certain to report to Tara. Not that he gave a damn about that, but it could bring Tara back to Wungalla—the last thing he wanted. There had been the small matter of finding a governess for Georgy, of course, but an agency could have sent him a competent young woman who didn't attract attention to herself unlike the blossoming Ms Devlin.

His mind continued to wander. She had fallen pregnant at age what, fifteen? Scarcely more than a child. He was ready to believe it had been against her will. She was so innocent looking, yet despite that so powerfully *alluring,* there were bound to have been men following her with hot, desirous eyes. Hadn't he threatened Pearson with instant dismissal if he even so much as glanced again in her direction? He imagined what life would have been like for her, a young girl, saddled with a child. What had happened to her lover after he had so callously dishonoured her? What of her family, the father she spoke of? She was well spoken, well educated, with the unmistakable look of good blood. Was her story much worse than his imaginings? What was she doing out here really? Trying to lose herself and the boy, on the run from some man? It was the kind of nightmare many women and children faced. Any such predator would be a fool to venture into *his* world after them. On Wungalla they were safe.

CHAPTER FIVE

MARISSA had only just arrived back at the homestead when Olly bustled into the entrance hall to tell her Mrs McMaster was feeling much better today and would like to meet her.

'Why the bare feet, love?' Olly asked, staring down at Marissa's feet in amazement.

'My shoes are wet. I left them out on the verandah. It's a long story, Olly. I'll tell you later. Meanwhile I'd better change these trousers for a skirt. They're damp around the hem.'

Olly lifted her brows. 'You found Holt?'

'He found *me*,' Marissa started to run up the staircase to hide her blushes. Besides, the last thing she wanted to do was keep Mrs McMaster waiting. 'It's okay for Georgy to shift down to our wing,' she called over her shoulder.

'I'll get right on it,' Olly said, 'after I take you along to Mrs McMaster. Georgy will be pleased. They've been as good as gold while you've been away. All Georgy wants to do is please Riley. He's an enormous improvement on Zoltan.'

Here's hoping it stays that way!

Catherine McMaster, Holt's paternal grandmother, was a diminutive, almost doll-like, old lady with abundant silvery-white hair, and hazel eyes that seemed to *glow* in her small, fine boned face. Her skin was relatively unlined, but paper thin, almost transparent. It was easy enough to see she must once have been a great beauty. At eighty-two she still possessed beauty, in one of its other forms. She was very lightly, but perfectly made up. She wore a lovely blue silk embroidered caftan over narrow white linen trousers, little white flatties, like ballet shoes on her feet. Her voice when she spoke was surprisingly strong and clear.

'Come over here, child. I want to look at you,' she ordered gently. Outback royalty she might be, but her manner was kind and friendly. Something for which Marissa was instantly grateful.

'I'm so pleased to meet you, Mrs McMaster,' Marissa said, doing as she was bid.

'And I to meet you.' The old lady remained standing near the open French doors, with brilliant sunlight spilling across the broad rear verandah. She put out her hand.

Marissa took it with great care. She feared crushing the thin, arthritic fingers and causing pain. 'Holt told me you were pretty but he didn't do you justice!' Catherine gave a dry chuckle. 'Deliberately, I think.' Her whole manner appeared brimming with interest.

Marissa smiled, but made no response. She had learned to take comments on her looks with a smile and a minimum of embarrassment. Her looks were so much a part of her it was difficult to feel self-conscious about them. But there *was* a downside. Sometimes those very looks caused her trouble, like Wade Pearson for instance. She'd had to avoid many a Wade in her time.

'Let's sit, shall we?' Catherine McMaster invited most winningly, still holding Marissa's hand. Marissa, in turn, guided the old lady to the comfortable looking day bed drawn up near the French doors. Catherine settled herself gingerly, a clear indication her bones ached. 'Thank you, my dear.' She still spoke with a pronounced English accent for all her many long years in Australia. Her grandson's voice had the same precision, Marissa thought. 'I tire easily these days. Just another one of the set-backs of old age. There's very little to recommend it.'

'I'm sorry if you're in pain,' Marissa said.

'One learns to live with it. It all comes down to acceptance.' Catherine gestured Marissa into the armchair nearby.

It was a beautiful, large, light filled room they were in, all white, the walls, the sheer curtains, the lovely bed coverings on the antique iron and bronze bed, the silk upholstery on the armchairs and Catherine's chaise longue. Colour came from silk cushions in an exquisite shade of blue, a collection of beautiful flower paintings in gold frames, and another fine collection of blue and white Chinese porcelain housed in a tall white cabinet. Nothing had a hard edge. It was all soft and dreamy. Marissa loved it.

Catherine noticed. She smiled, 'You like my room?'

'I *love* it!' There was no mistaking Marissa's sincerity. 'There's an absolute peace about it. It's a beautiful retreat.'

'I've always had an affinity for white,' Catherine said. 'I grew up in a house that had the most beautiful garden. People used to come from all over to see it. I have pictures of it somewhere I must show you. In one section of the garden all the flowers were white. Do you like gardens?'

'How could I not!' Marissa smiled. 'Since they never fail to give pleasure. Gardens are very special places. They add so much to our sense of place, don't you think?'

Catherine nodded in agreement. 'Indeed I do.' They spoke for a while about their favourite flowers, finding a shared taste. Catherine allowed the young woman to talk happily. Holt had told her Marissa had brought a child with her, a little boy of seven who miraculously had bonded with Georgia. The young woman claimed the boy was her half brother. Holt had somehow formed the opinion the boy was her son.

Many things happened in life, Catherine thought. Good things. Bad things. She wasn't about to steamroll her way into this young woman's most private areas. The full story would come in its own good time.

'You can imagine what a job I had getting a garden going here,' Catherine declared. 'I had enormous help from a dear friend. He wasn't a professional landscaper but he might well have been. We planned Wungalla's home gardens together.'

'And they're magnificent!' Marissa could see the great spreading trees outside. 'I've seen the park in Ransom. The jacarandas are in bloom right now, a glorious sight. Deidre O'Connell told me you were responsible for the park, how you had it developed and the jacarandas planted.'

'And haven't they thrived!' Catherine said with immense satisfaction. 'Though I haven't seen the park in many a day.'

'One of my earliest memories is of jacarandas in bloom,' Marissa confided in a dreamlike voice as though she had just suddenly remembered. 'In those days we had a beautiful old colonial. It sat on top of a hill with 360-degree views. The house was surrounded by huge jacarandas. For the short time they were in bloom it was paradise. Then the summer storms always came to blow the blossom away like the cherry blossom in Japan.' Unconsciously her expression had saddened, something that wasn't lost on Catherine.

'How old were you when you shifted house?' Catherine asked gently. 'This was in Brisbane?'

'Yes.' Marissa nodded, gathering herself. 'I would have been eight.' The days when she was happy; the days when her father had often declared himself to be 'the happiest man in the world.' Marissa kept her voice steady. 'A few years later my mother was killed in a car accident. My father was at the wheel.'

'And he blamed himself terribly,' Catherine supplied in a quiet understanding voice, seeing the young woman was having difficulty going on. The traumatisation had included father and daughter. 'I'm so sorry, Marissa,' she said. 'I understand the pain doesn't go away. I lost my husband, a giant of a man, then my son, Holt's father. I was stoic at the death of my husband. I had to carry on. I was like a mad woman after I lost my son. My only consolation is *I'll* go long before my Holt.'

'Please, don't go, Mrs McMaster,' Marissa found herself saying in a heartfelt voice. 'I want us to be friends.'

Catherine's eyes sparkled. 'And we will be, I'm sure. I must meet this young brother of yours, Riley. That *is* his name?'

Someone actually believed her! Marissa's smile lent radiance to her face. 'Yes. He's a lovely boy with a strong bright character. He won't be any trouble. In fact he and Georgy appear to have formed an instant bond.'

'So I've heard! Due no doubt to something angelic in Riley's nature. Georgy has suffered as any child would suffer as *you* did, my dear, from the loss of a mother. Your mother and I'm sure you loved her greatly was *taken* from you. Georgy's mother gave her away. Holt has been wonderful through it all. No one—and I include myself—was fully aware of Tara's true nature. A lot was kept from us, but this abandonment was what turned

Georgy into the willful capricious child she has been up to date. If yours and Riley's influence can calm her, I'm certain we can expect better things.'

Marissa left Catherine's bedroom feeling very much happier in herself. She had not been expecting the—from all accounts formidable Mrs McMaster—to be so kindly and so approachable. They had talked easily, their conversation covering a range of subjects apart from the gardens they both loved. It was discovered they took joy in the same things. Books, music, poetry which they both thought very neglected and what Marissa found absolutely enthralling, Catherine's recollections of what it had felt like coming as a young bride to a strange, new country so very different from her own. It hadn't been a case of her transplanting fairly easily to one of the major cities where she would have lived a life far more in keeping with the one she had left. Madly in love she had broken the ties of love and blood that held her to her beloved parents and her own country, to take on the daunting task of becoming mistress of a vast Australian Outback cattle station. Her family at home had widely believed given the isolation, and the 'savagery' of her new environment the marriage would fail.

The marriage had not only endured; it had thrived

through every set-back, every obstacle—through pitiless drought, and raging floods, family tragedies, station tragedies. Wungalla to everyone's amazement became Catherine's passion. She was a coloniser; a woman who put down dynastic roots. Small wonder she was widely regarded as being a great lady, a true pioneer.

Marissa had found comfort in being around her. A woman of such wisdom and experience offered spiritual balm. Marissa felt in need of it. Her own happy family life had come to an end with the death of her mother. Marissa still desperately missed her. For her father after her mother's passing there had been *no* glimmer of light. He must have experienced short bursts of feeling human after Riley was born she thought, impossible to be around Riley and *not* feel the light. Hadn't little Georgy, abandoned by her mother, responded to that light of Riley's slanting over her?

A few days later—extremely uncomfortable days for Marissa when she had to come into contact with Lois at dinner—Holt elected to fly Lois to Sydney himself.

'I don't want you having to go to the bother of organising a charter flight,' he told her smoothly. 'I have business I can attend to while I'm there, so it's no problem.' He turned his shoulders slightly as he waited for her answer.

Marissa feared there would have been an explosion only for Catherine's gracious presence at the dinner table. Marissa had supervised the children's tea well over an hour before, now she had joined them in the breakfast room off the kitchen, where the family ate their meals when they weren't entertaining. The formal dining room was much too big and too grand, for day-to-day living. Which wasn't to say the 'breakfast' room wasn't enormously pleasing. It opened directly onto the rear garden allowing the scents to waft in. She liked the way it was furnished, as well, with comfortable rattan chairs upholstered in turquoise and white set down a long refectory table that allowed plenty of room for everyone and the array of dishes Olly served. A timber sideboard even longer than the table held tea and coffee and the various offerings Olly set out for breakfast at which times they helped themselves. The room's close proximity to the kitchen made Olly's work very much easier although she had many a helping hand in the form of the house girls who moved about quiet as shadows. Marissa had attempted conversation but so far their responses had been confined to muffled giggles and shy smiles.

Lois was taking her time answering, staring down into her half empty wineglass as though at the bottom lay her answer. 'It sounds like you want to get rid of me.' she said finally, a throb in her voice.

It was Catherine who answered, looking distressed. 'No, no, Lois. That's not it at all. You've been so good giving Georgia your time and attention, but you must be missing city life. I'm sure your friends are missing you.'

Lois blinked rapidly, perhaps fighting back tears. 'You're very kind, Mrs McMaster, but I *feel* like I have to go. In fact I feel like I'll never be invited to this house again.'

'Oh, for God's sake, Lois!' Holt showed his impatience with histrionics. Clearly he had seen too much of it. 'I *swear* I will invite you. Have no fear. I didn't realise you found Outback life so fascinating. You never have in the past.'

'Tara never wanted me here,' she said.

Because she knew you were in love with her husband.

Marissa looked away, hating to be caught in the middle of this. Couldn't Lois have waited to speak to Holt privately?

'Tara, I believe, is overseas. Is that right?' he asked, his expression sufficient for anyone to change the subject.

Lois nodded slowly. 'She'll be home soon. She's in Dubai at the moment. Loves it!'

'Probably catching up on her shopping,' Holt said suavely. 'Don't you want to see her? She's most likely brought you back something you don't want.'

Lois threw down her napkin. 'I *hate* you, Holt,' she cried, her tongue loosened by the wine.

'Well, it's better than loving me,' he said.

'Holt!' Catherine shot her beloved grandson, a swift, reproving glance.

'Look I don't want to upset you, Lois,' he responded to that glance with a much more conciliatory tone, 'but I think we've reached a point where you'd be happier back home. I assure you we are looking forward to having you back at Christmas.'

'Oh, shut up!' Lois wailed, jumping to her feet. 'It's all *this one's* fault, isn't it?' She stabbed an accusing finger at the mortified Marissa. 'I've worked so hard, done so much but I haven't been appreciated. Mark my words *this one* will turn out to be worse than the other two.'

'*This one's* name is Marissa,' Holt stressed. 'And I'm determined to give her a fighting chance. You're upsetting Gran, Lois. I won't have that. I was enjoying having her company at dinner.'

Lois looked like she'd been slapped across the

face. 'I'm so sorry, Mrs McMaster,' she apologised hastily. 'I don't know what's got into me.'

'You're very uptight, Lois,' Catherine said quietly. 'Sometimes the isolation can strain one's nerves. And there's no denying Georgy has been quite a handful. We very much appreciate what you've tried to do. Please, sit down again, dear. I don't like to see *you* upset. But you mustn't upset Marissa, either. She doesn't deserve it.'

Incredibly Lois gave way to a gale of bitter laughter. 'You're not getting *any* of this, are you?'

'Yes, I *am*, Lois,' Catherine said, for a fraction of a second showing her anger. 'We will excuse you if you would like.'

Lois thrust her chair back, heading for the door. She was almost there, when she turned. 'How can you trust her?' she demanded of Holt looking directly at him. 'Do you really need a person like that to teach Georgia, to live in your house? Have you even bothered to check out her background? I bet she's got plenty to hide.'

The strain of Lois's antagonism finally caught up with Marissa. She closed her eyes, then opened them quickly. 'I don't have a police record, Ms Aldridge,' she said. 'I've done nothing unlawful in my life. I've presented Mr McMaster with my references. They're excellent. I'm well qualified to teach your niece.'

'And there's *more!*' Holt leaned back in his chair. 'She could probably teach you a thing or two, Lois.'

Lois wasn't about to let that go by. 'Nothing I'd *want* to learn!' she hurled at him, before stalking off.

There was a long pause while they all waited for the clack of Lois's high heels on the marble tiles to fade away.

'Oh, dear, oh, dear, oh, dear,' Catherine softly moaned. 'When was the last time Lois put on a turn like that? It must be what, two or three years?'

'I believe it was around the time of the divorce,' Holt said his handsome face as unyielding as rock.

'She does have her nose out of joint,' Catherine said, fully realising Lois felt threatened by the presence of a beautiful young woman at *Wungalla*. 'Did you really have to goad her, my darling?'

'Goad her?' Holt's fine white teeth clenched. 'Good God, Gran, she was out on the attack. She didn't give a damn if she upset you, or Marissa. In fact I think she was aching to get it off her chest.'

'Would you like me to leave?' Marissa asked quickly, looking first at Catherine, then Holt.

'Why should you?' he countered, impatiently. 'You haven't finished your meal. Neither have I. Gran has, no problem there.'

'Stay, dear,' Catherine urged Marissa, giving a little shake of her hand. 'I suppose there's no point in going after Lois?' she asked of no one in particular.

'No point at all,' Holt confirmed shortly. 'She'll cool off by morning. *Did* she upset you?' He looked at his grandmother keenly.

'Not really, darling,' Catherine answered a little too quickly. 'But I do think I might retire now. I was so enjoying being with you right up to the moment you suggested flying Lois home. Though I'm sure it's the right thing.'

'It is from where I'm standing,' Holt said, getting to his feet. 'Come on now, sweetheart, I'll take you upstairs.'

Marissa had never thought to hear him speak so tenderly. He was such a complicated man, very difficult to get used to.

'Thank you, darling.' Catherine's hazel eyes met Marissa's. 'Try to excuse Lois, my dear. Sad to say, you've awakened the not so nice side of her. Lois can be charming and she *has* tried with Georgy.'

'Or we're going to *pretend* she did,' Holt said. 'Want me to carry you?'

'Your grandfather used to,' Catherine said, looking way up at him with twinkling eyes.

'And I'm not the man to run away from a challenge, either!' He swept his doll-like grand-mother off her feet, pausing only to tell Marissa to stay put.

A moment or two later, Olly who had obviously heard raised voices—perhaps even listened in?—came through the kitchen door.

'What was that all about?' she asked in a con-spiratorial whisper. It was obvious right from the beginning she felt free to ask questions of Marissa.

Marissa took a deep breath. Lois mightn't be thrilled about her presence on Wungalla, but Olly was treating her as if she were a bona fide member of the family and not the new governess. 'Holt offered to fly Lois back to Sydney.'

'*Ooooh!'* Olly staggered back against the side-board. 'So that's what it was all about. I bet she took it badly?'

'Very,' Marissa said, feeling largely to blame.

'I just hope she didn't upset Mrs McMaster,' Olly rallied, jamming her hands into the wide front pocket of her apron. 'She really has made an effort to come downstairs for dinner. She likes you, love.'

That made Marissa feel better. 'Well, I like *her,'* she exclaimed rather emotionally. 'I would *love* to have a grandmother like that.'

'But what about your own grandmothers?' Olly

prompted. She had formed the definite opinion—
and she was rarely wrong—Marissa had braved
her way through a dysfunctional childhood into
adolescence and young womanhood. Talking about
it might take a lot of pressure off her Olly reasoned.

Marissa allowed her mind to range back to the
beginning of the bad times. 'My maternal grandmother was lovely, but she was *shattered* when my
mother was killed. She turned overnight into a
different woman. It took her years and years to
recover. In fact she never did. She's dead now. My
father's mother had a very full social life. Neither
of them was in the position to take on a grieving
child. My uncle Bryan, my father's brother and his
wife, Allison, reared me. I lived with them until I
started University. After that, I lived on campus in
a women's college.'

'Uncle Bryan and Aunt Allison, were they good
people?' Olly didn't want to be too pushy but
there were things she wanted to know. Marissa
and young Riley were already weaving tendrils
around her heart.

Marissa met Olly's shrewd but kindly eyes.
'Uncle Bryan is a good, conscientious man. He did
his best for me.'

'And Aunt Allison?' Olly had her first glimmering
of what Marissa's home life might have been like.

'She did her best, too,' Marissa said briefly.

'And your dad?' Olly rushed in where angels fear to tread.

But Marissa couldn't talk about it. She feared bursting into tears. 'I'm sorry, Olly.' She shook her head. 'I can't go there. There's too much pain. Maybe when I—'

'Now, now, I understand, love,' Olly broke in, cursing herself for speaking too soon. 'You've let your meal go cold.' She clicked her tongue looking at Marissa's half empty plate. She had served up a beautiful roast beef fillet wrapped in prosciutto with potato gratin and fresh green peas 'There's plenty more in the kitchen.'

'And it was lovely, too, Olly. But really I'm fine. You're a wonderful cook. Perhaps some time when you're in the mood you could give me a few lessons. I've done a lot of study in my time but I've never had cooking lessons. Aunt Ally wouldn't let me anywhere near the kitchen except for the cleanup jobs and emptying the dishwasher. She *hated* that. So did Lucy.'

Olly sank into a chair, her face bent across the table. 'And Lucy was?'

'My cousin. Lucy is two years older than I am.'

'I would have expected you to be good friends?'

'We weren't friends from the start,' Marissa said.

'I expect a lot of it was my fault. They were very painful times. I spent a lot of time battling tears.'

'Nothing unusual about that, love,' Olly said softly.

Marissa lowered her head. 'I didn't storm around the place like Georgy may do in an effort to contain her pain. I didn't shout or swear or pick fights with Lucy. I didn't tell anyone I hated them. I might as well have. My aunt told me frequently I was a selfish, ungrateful girl.'

'She sounds like a perfect horror!' Olly said indignantly.

Marissa reacted by laughing. 'She *was,* you know,' she said, marvelling someone had finally put it into words. 'Because of her mother Lucy had difficulties with me. I think now, we both suffered. But enough of that! I don't usually talk about myself.'

'You've got to let yourself go now and again, love,' Olly advised, getting to her feet again. 'You can't always bottle it up.'

'I've come to believe in the power of silence, Olly,' Marissa said.

As well she might!

Holt had been standing a while outside the doorway listening unashamedly to the conversation. He fully understood Olly's efforts to get the new governess to talk. The strange part was, so great was Marissa's appeal, not only his grand-mother and Olly were starting to worry about her, so was *he!* It was even difficult to think about her as an employee. She was more like a young family member who had sought refuge on Wungalla. He'd have to stop her calling him Mr McMaster, correct though it might be. He didn't like the sound of it on her lips.

'Good evening!' he greeted them satirically, walking back into the room.

'And good evening to you, too, *sor,*' Olly responded with a thick Irish brogue. 'How's Mrs McMaster?'

'She's settled. I expect you heard the ruckus?'

Olly's eyes shifted to Marissa. 'I'd have been deaf *not* to,' she said. 'Such a shame when Mrs McMaster had been enjoying herself.'

'There'll be other nights, Olly.' Holt glanced down at Marissa's silky head, a mass of waves and curls. 'You okay?'

'I'm fine, thank you,' she answered, very politely. She didn't twist her head to look up at him.

'In that case you'll be ready for the next course.' He resumed his seat, opposite her, tossing off the last of the fine red in his wine-glass. 'I would have thought good manners required not starting a fight at the dinner table, but how times do change! What's for dessert, Olly?' he asked.

'Those little ricotta fritters you like with a citrus sauce,' she answered with satisfaction.

He waved a hand. 'Perfect! Bring them on. My nerves need soothing.'

'Will do!' Olly laughed and walked away.

Marissa, feeling at her most vulnerable, began to fold her napkin, uncertain what to do next.

'You're not going anywhere surely?' His brilliant black eyes pinned her in place. 'I thought I told you to stay.'

'Well, *I* thought probably my being here had something to do with your frayed nerves?' she found herself saying.

He stared at her for some time. 'You know you're *right!* But let me worry about that. Have dessert, maybe a coffee, afterwards we can take a turn in the garden.'

Her heart fluttered like a bird, right up into her throat. 'Isn't that a bit social for a governess?'

He took his time considering. 'Do you know, I think it *is,* but you seem to have transformed yourself into a little friend of the family. My grandmother is quite taken with you. That's not always the case. It's certainly not in the contract. And you and Olly are into sharing secrets.'

She could feel herself flush. 'How do *you* know?'

He leaned forward, giving her a slow, mocking smile. 'This *is* my house, Ms Devlin I have no compunction whatever about eavesdropping.'

Simply for something to do, she started to drum her fingernails against the timber table. 'I'll have to remember that.'

'Then I shouldn't have told you. Can you do that while rubbing the top of your head?'

'What?' Completely thrown, she stared back at him. My God he was handsome!

'*I* can,' he said. 'Perfect co-ordination.' He began to drum the fingers of his right hand on the table while with his other hand he circled the top of her head.

'Easy!' She took up the challenge, thinking she would have the children try it.

That was how Olly found them.

Marissa checked on the children; found them soundly asleep, before going back downstairs. Going for an after dinner stroll with the master of Wungalla she thought a bit over the top, but he'd insisted and she needed this job. Besides, he knew perfectly well the way he made her feel. Not that she was going to allow her quite under-standable susceptibilities to get out of hand. She was certain Holt McMaster was used to a great deal of female attention.

Had he gone for evening strolls with the previous governesses? she wondered. If so no wonder they got wild ideas into their heads. Had he and Lois taken nightly walks beneath the glorious Outback stars? Poor desperately angry and hurt, Lois. Had Lois been led down the metaphoric garden path? Were they, in fact, lovers? A man like that with such a powerful sexual aura, was hardly likely to have remained celibate after his divorce. Were there other lovers tucked away? Quite likely. But weren't men always going on about a male heir? He would remarry. Running a vast cattle station was a man's job in a man's world.

'Do we keep to the path?' Her voice sounded composed, but her nerves were jingling.

'Absolutely! The straight and narrow,' he confirmed.

'Did you ask my predecessors to take an after-dinner stroll?' The words left her mouth before she had time to call them back.

He looked down his dead straight nose at her. 'Just because I asked *you* doesn't mean I've asked others, Ms Devlin.'

'I'm sorry. Should I be flattered, Mr McMaster?'

'You're not supposed to be anything!' he told her

crisply. 'Just enjoy the stars and the night air. By the way you can drop the Mr McMaster.'

'So soon?' How the man loosened her tongue!

'You know, Ms Devlin, I'm concerned at the way you're starting to question what I say.'

The truth of that jolted her. She attempted an explanation. 'It's only because you go out of your way to make me feel uncomfortable.'

'How?' He moved a long sweeping frond away from her face.

'I don't really know my position.'

'More or less governess,' he said. 'I'll always try to think of you that way. I can't answer for my grandmother. You did tell her you'd read to her?'

'Of course I will!' She stared up at him, seeing him clearly in the glow from the exterior lights. 'I'd be delighted to. I don't say things I don't mean.'

'How I wish I could say the same of myself,' he said dryly, taking hold of her elbow momentarily while he steered her onto a branching path. 'I'm taking Lois back with me tomorrow. We'll leave right after an early breakfast. I'm not asking you to run down and join us. I'll be gone for several days, probably a week.'

'I take it I'm in charge of the schoolroom?' Her leaping nerves had gone haywire when he touched her. How could just the touch of a hand do that?

'I could scarcely put you in charge of anything else. Gran told me you ride? I'd appreciate your being absolutely honest about this. You *ride,* or you can just about manage to stay on a very quiet horse?'

She had to move closer to him as the branching foliage reached for her. 'I love the way you put things. I suppose I could say in all modesty I'm a good rider. My father bought me my first pony when I was five. He—' She stopped abruptly, her memories clinging to her like a second skin.

'And I hate it when you do that,' he said. 'Go on.'

'I've said enough.' She shook her head. 'I've answered the question. Riley can ride, as well. Both of us are what you call naturals. We love horses.'

'Well, of course! We inherit our tastes. Georgy you will find has a fear of horses. She had a bad experience when she was quite small. Much the same thing happened at the pool. She fears the water.'

'That's sad.' Was it possible he had thrown the child in at the deep end? She had heard of a few fathers who did that, genuinely believing their child would somehow miraculously swim. She couldn't see Holt McMaster doing it—certainly not to a little girl—though she wished he would reach out more to his child. He seemed more like a laid-back, affectionate uncle than a father. 'A few things have occurred to me that might cure that. I promise I would take things slowly. I understand children's fears. Riley will be a big help. Like me he's a good swimmer.'

'Did you teach him?'

She pushed her windswept hair away from her face. 'No, I didn't.'

He glanced down at her. She was wearing a silvery little blouse she must have had tucked away somewhere in her travel-light luggage. It looked expensive. It suited her. Oddly he had an idea he had seen it before. If it did turn out she *was* a single mother on the run she still managed to retain a look of exclusivity. Ms Marissa Devlin had a story to tell. One, he found, he badly wanted to hear. He knew he could have her background checked in a minute, but something in him shied away from that. He wanted to hear it from her own lips.

'So who did?' he asked finally.

'My father.' Marissa started to retreat automatically, but found herself adding. 'He taught Riley lots of things.'

'He did well. Riley's a great little guy.'

'I think so.'

The enchanted indigo-blue night and the brilliance of the stars should have soothed her, but however hard she tried, she had to accept she was succumbing to this man's black magic. And it *was* magic. Like so many others before her, she was falling for it.

'You haven't asked me anything about my teaching methods?' she said. 'Or told me if there's any subject in particular you want me to work on with Georgy?'

There was a torched pause. 'Best of all, Ms Devlin, I'd like you to work on her day-to-day behaviour although I have to say whatever system you have in place it's having great results. You did allow me to see your excellent reference from the worthy Doctor Bell, wasn't it?'

'Yes, my friend and my mentor. She did everything she could to make life easier. At school at least.'

'What exactly was wrong with your home life?'

'Nothing was really wrong. It was just that I was looking for love.'

'Aren't we all?'

His answer surprised her. Why? Because he appeared so utterly self-contained? 'Forgive me if I'm out of line but your divorce must have been very painful. For you and for Georgy.'

He glanced down at her, his tone sardonic. 'When you say you're out of line, you *are,* Ms Devlin.'

'But you can ask me anything you like?'

'Now don't sound miffed. That's different, isn't it?'

'Sorry.' She forced her breath to stay even. They were moving through an avenue of shrubs freighted with fragrant blossom, but it was darker here, more mysterious, the only light that pouring out of the starry sky.

'I suppose the best way I could describe my divorce was, a tremendous *relief,*' he said. 'The truth, I believe, is always best.'

Was that another dig at her? 'You'd fallen totally out of love?' She couldn't keep a little lick of reproof out of her voice.

'I think we might start with *your* big love affair?' he countered suavely. 'Unless you prefer not to discuss it?'

'Do you know I've never had a big love affair.'

'That's hard to believe,' he said.

'Riley is *not* my child.'

He stopped on the path, and turned her towards him. 'So you say, but he plays your son to perfection.'

'Is that so unusual in a little boy who…'

She knew she had a real problem talking about this, even to save herself and her reputation. She couldn't bring herself to talk about her brilliant father's descent into the hell of alcoholism, plagued as she was by the feeling she might burst into tears. She couldn't bring herself to speak about the misery of his wasted life; the brief, failed relationship with Riley's runaway mother. She and Riley were having a bad enough time trying to cope with his death, both of them orphans of the storm.

'Okay,' he said gently, registering the tremble that shook her. 'We'd better walk back.'

She could still feel the imprint of his warm hands on her shoulders, searing the silk. 'I didn't lie to you,' she said after a moment.

'Just tell me this.' His voice was filled with real gravity. 'Are you afraid of someone?'

For one crazy moment she nearly burst out: you! *I'm afraid of you and your effect on me.* This was a man who literally took her breath away.

To Holt her long pause appeared like a dead give-away.

She managed a low, tremulous, 'No!'

'You and Riley are quite safe on Wungalla.'

'I know that. You've been very kind.'

'And here I was thinking you hadn't noticed.' His tone was at its most mocking.

They were walking beneath the canopy of tall trees when suddenly, with a screech as loud as a klaxon, a large bird swooped from its dark green cover appearing to make a dive for them.

Immediately Holt swung up an arm, while with the other he pulled the cowering Marissa to his side where she buried her head. 'Get! Go on, get!' he shouted at the bird.

With another screech, the bird was gone, flapping its wings heavily as it flew across the garden.

'My God, what was it, an eagle?' Marissa felt safe enough to lift her face.

'Don't be silly!' He laughed, adding insult to injury. 'An eagle wouldn't be nesting in those trees. A wedge tailed eagle has a wingspan of over seven feet. An eagle could have picked you up and carried you away to its desert eyrie.'

'I only meant it was *huge!*' she said, defending herself. She was leaning against him and he still had one arm around her.

Holt tried hard to collect his thoughts. They were flowing through him like a stream in flood. The only way he could fight back temptation was to stay perfectly still. He had never in his life met a woman he so wanted to pick up and carry off. For long moments she had been snuggling against him, hiding her silky head against his chest. He wasn't starving for sex. He knew he could get it whether or not he proposed marriage—but he was starving for sex with the *right* woman. One that moved him, tore at his heart. One he had *wanted* on sight. The great irony was he had no option but to restrain all his wild impulses. She and the boy were under his protection.

He released her carelessly. 'Sorry the bird spooked you, but I think it's safe to walk you home.'

Some note in his voice created the illusion that was what he meant.

Home.

She didn't know if she would ever find one but Wungalla was the next best thing.

CHAPTER SIX

BY THE end of a week Marissa had established a workable routine. It hadn't been entirely plain sailing. Georgy still gave in to the odd moment when she had to get a good lusty shout out of her system, but there were no screams, no tantrums. Instead day by day she blossomed into a bright happy co-operative child.

'It's your gentle, understanding hand, Marissa, my dear,' Catherine told her. 'You must make lessons interesting, too. I always knew Georgy was highly intelligent, but no one could have called her an apt pupil. The last governess was at her wit's end.'

To Marissa's mind, Riley pointed out the probable answer. 'I must be like one of those quiet little ponies trainers use to keep their thoroughbreds calm before the races.' He gave his infectious laugh, causing Georgy, who was most interested in the theory, to join in.

'Well, I know about that, but how do you?'

Marissa asked, constantly surprised by Riley's fund of general knowledge.

Riley's response was instant. 'Daddy told me.' For the first time he didn't sound distressed when he mentioned their father. 'He even took me to the country races once. We had a great time. Do they have country races here?' He turned to Georgy with a look of happy expectancy.

'We have better!' she pronounced, jumping up from her desk and waving her arms expansively. 'We have polo matches. Holt is a beaut player! My mother used to call him The Conqueror. I think that means he used to hit other players on the conk with his mallet, but he didn't. Last year it was Wungalla's turn to host the final. We had the Polo Ball in the Great Hall. I didn't get to go on account of being small, but my aunties came. They're really nice to me. Aunty Alex was Holt's hostess seeing I don't have a mum. She did a great job. Aunty Lois came, as well. She's head over heels in love with Holt but he won't commit.'

Marissa stared at the little girl intently. 'Who did you hear say that, Georgy?'

Georgy's face settled into a wicked grin. 'How do you know I didn't say it myself?'

'They're the words of an adult,' Marissa replied,

'and they really shouldn't be repeated. They can only cause embarrassment. Do you know what embarrassment means?'

Georgy shrugged her thin shoulders. 'It'd make Aunty Lois mad of course. *Ack-shally,* it was Aunt Lois's friend, Tiffany. The one she brought with her from Sydney. Are we ever going to see Aunt Lois again?' She directed that question at Marissa who responded warmly.

'Well, of course you are! Aunt Lois is family. I understand she'll be here at Christmas.'

'Just so long as you two guys are!' said Georgy. 'Riley can marry me when we grow up.'

Riley gulped.

'You can sit down now, Georgy,' Marissa said. 'For now, we have to get cracking on your sums.'

'Can Riley help me?' Georgy returned obediently to her desk.

Most late afternoons Marissa and Riley enjoyed a swim. Georgy had begun by sitting on one of the recliners, gradually moving closer to the pool, until finally she chose to sit on the top step at the shallow end dangling her feet in the water.

'Why don't you come in?' Riley called, his eyes the brightest blue in his glowing face. 'It's great! I'll look after you.'

'Don't pressure her, Riley.' Marissa swam up behind him speaking very quietly.

'I don't have a swimsuit,' Georgy called. It didn't sound like an excuse, rather regret.

'Don't worry, we'll get one,' Marissa called back. 'Something really smart. Your father will be home Sunday.'

'Are you going to tell him I'm cured?' The expression on Georgy's small face was one of hope.

'Cured of *what?*' Riley lifted himself out of the water to sit on the step beside her.

'Cured of being frightened of the water,' she told him simply. 'My mother was always trying to throw me in the pool. She was really mean, like *your* mum.'

Marissa's heart lurched. The children were growing close. They spent quite a lot of time talking to one another. From the sound of it Riley had been confiding in his new friend. She had to consider it as therapy. At least Georgy had accepted she wasn't Riley's mother.

'After you teach me how to swim, you have to teach me how to sit on a horse,' Georgy further astounded them by saying.

'And you have to teach me to draw pictures as good as yours,' Riley said.

'You *like* my pictures?' Georgy looked at him in amazement, her cheeks going quite pink.

'Very, very much!' said Riley.

Georgy started cracking her knuckles. 'Well, Aunty Lois said she should show them to a psy… psy…'

'Psychiatrist,' Riley sweetly supplied. 'Maybe you have way too much imagination for her?'

Georgy kissed him. 'After tea I'm going to sing for you. You and Marissa. You're my *great* friends. I have a really good voice but only Zoltan ever heard it.'

'What songs do you know then?' Riley eyed her with admiration.

Georgy jumped up so she could hand Marissa her towel. 'Wait and see.'

If they were expecting nursery ditties, Twinkle, Twinkle, Little Star, Rudolph the Red-Nosed Reindeer, Click Go the Shears, Boy, Tom, Tom the Piper's Son and the like, Georgy's performance brought the house down. She had graciously consented to give her impromptu concert in her great-grandmother's sitting room.

The pint-size performer began by introducing the first of two songs from her repertoire before she sang them.

Nothing like 'Danny Boy' to bring on the tears, especially when sung in a pure sweet pipe. Then to end the concert on an upbeat note, one of her favourites from *The Sound of Music* complete with a really good natural yodel.

'Julie Andrews couldn't have done it any better,' Olly pronounced, admitting later it had never crossed her mind Georgy could sing. Shriek, yes, sing like a lark, no.

Catherine gave the child a lovely smile. 'That was absolutely beautiful, Georgy. Thank you so much.'

'I'm going to be a singer when I grow up,' Georgy told her charmed audience. 'I think singing to people would be great!'

Holt arrived home to a contented household. After some harrowing moments with Lois, whose undying, let it be said, *unrequited,* love for him, had been wrung out of her, it was the peaceful homecoming he needed. Why was it that some women insisted on falling in love with the one man they couldn't have? Of course he had long known about Lois's feelings for him. How could he not? Tara had been very cruel in the way she had privately ridiculed her sister. Even when he had objected quite strongly she had invariably replied, 'It just makes me laugh, darling, that's all! You're *mine,* so just don't forget it!'

But it was Tara who had broken their marriage

vows. With a minor rock star of all people! A good-looking young guy, years younger than she who had been part of a band hired to play at a friend's wedding reception in Sydney. He and his father had been out of the country at the time, as members of a trade commission. Had he been home it would never have happened. But Tara when she was in the mood, just *had* to have sex. The big problem was the rock star hadn't been using a condom and the one thing Tara hadn't figured on happening, happened. She had fallen pregnant with Georgia.

The truly extraordinary part was she hadn't considered herself unfaithful. She hadn't felt in the least guilty about what other people called adultery. It might well have been an out-of-body experience, something over which she had little control.

'He meant *nothing!* Less than nothing, darling. Just a good-looking kid in skintight jeans. I was drunk, darling! It was a wild, wild night! He must have slipped me something when I wasn't noticing.'

The marriage hadn't come to an end right then. Not in name anyway, although he'd never touched her again. The truth was he had discovered very early in their marriage Tara wasn't the young woman he'd so stupidly thought she was. Tara, his beautiful, charming fiancée had been playing a part, like an actress in a movie. She'd been so good at it she had fooled his entire family, except maybe for Gran, who had once tried to warn him by saying, 'Tara is lovely, Holt, but not quite *believable!*'

Tara's parents knew all about their very difficult elder daughter and her wildly fluctuating moods. So did Lois, but none of them had been interested in telling him. Tara was unstable in more ways than one. It was this instability that had caused him much worry about Georgia. It seemed very much as if she'd inherited her mother's nature. But he had only been home a few days to find Georgia was behaving like a normal happy child. It gladdened his heart that she had been spared.

Marissa had told him about Georgia's amazing talent for singing, clearly expecting him to demand to hear her that very moment. When he had declined saying it would have to wait until he had a little more time, he had caught the flash of disappointment and yes, *censure,* in her beautiful eyes. Clearly she thought he wasn't much of a father. He didn't much like it. But then, she was a young woman who was trying to deal with a lot of hangups of her own. Both of them had one thing in common. They had chosen faithless partners.

What was he supposed to say anyway? 'I'm

doing my level best, *Ms Devlin*—a deliberate plot to try to keep her at a distance?—I'm very fond of Georgy. I support her in every way I can, but I'm only human. *Georgia's not mine!'*

He had spent a lot of time wondering whether the rock star should at least be told he had a daughter. He knew *he* would want to know if somewhere in the world a child of his existed. He would *owe* that child, his own flesh and blood. The one and only time he had spoken to Tara about it had set off a near psychotic episode. She had become hysterical, smashing things, valuable things. No one was to *ever* know. She had taken it completely for granted *he* would do the best for Georgia as he had supported her right through her pregnancy.

But no way was he going to remain married to her.

That had precipitated another crisis but he had been adamant. He wanted a divorce.

The upshot was Tara had left Wungalla in a blind fury. She had left him with her child. *I don't want the ugly little thing! I never wanted her. She was an appalling accident. You keep her you're so bloody sanctimonious!*

Tara had left, feeling utterly secure in her belief he would remain silent on the issue of Georgia's paternity. In many ways it was a dilemma. He didn't believe he should live a lie. He didn't believe Georgia should be denied the truth. But at what stage should he tell her?

A dilemma indeed, with the blue-eyed, so innocent looking Ms Devlin looking at him with naked reproach in her eyes when he was a man long used to respect.

Holt surprised them one afternoon by coming back with Dusty, saying he was going to take them all to the Blue Lotus lagoon, a permanent water hole on the station where the sacred water lilies were out in all their glory. Dusty, back in his element as a working dog, got very excited around Marissa and the children. Holt allowed them to play for a few moments then he brought Dusty to heel with a firm, 'Sit, boy!'

Dusty did, thumping his tail good-naturedly, a grin all over his face.

'Oh, this is such fun!' Georgy trilled, clapping her hands together. 'Isn't Dusty beautiful? I always wanted a dog. Riley is going to teach me to swim, Dad, when you get me some propers swimmers. Marissa said you would.'

'And she was absolutely right.' Holt opened the doors of the 4WD, his heart breaking a little at the sound of that 'Dad.' Georgy rarely called him Dad and he had to admit he hadn't encouraged it. 'Okay, pile in.'

Marissa who adored the bush and had made a few early morning forays on her own when the children were still asleep, found the Blue Lotus lagoon a place of magic right in the heart of the red plains country. It was sheltered from the desert winds by towering river gums and an under canopy of feathery acacias their branches interlacing. The large lagoon was a shining dark green with great patches of the lavender-blue water lilies holding their long exquisite heads above the surface of the water and their glossy pads. It was a wonderfully cool green world in great contrast to the sun scorched plains.

Marissa hovered at the top of the grassy slope while the children accompanied by a romping Dusty took off for the sandy banks that surrounded the long near moon-shaped lagoon.

Holt, standing midway, turned back to her, unwilling to reveal how the sight of her, the sound of her, was a source of great pleasure to him. He had *missed* seeing her all the time he'd been away. Which just served to show what a sterile thing his life had become when really his working life had a lot of drama.

Face it. He wanted a wife. Not a stepmother for Georgy. He wanted a woman for *him*. This young woman, Marissa, was living, eating, sleeping, working, breathing, under his roof. He had become used to seeing her every day. His grandmother was deriving comfort and pleasure from her company. Georgy was a different child. Olly sang her praises, saying she was going to develop into a 'great little cook.' That was the top of the ladder for Olly and fine by him. The atmosphere at the homestead these days was one of joyous *ease*. He could scarcely believe it. Surely something had to go wrong!

'Are you coming down?'

Under his brilliant gaze Marissa felt momentarily paralysed. Ever since he had come home she had been fighting down the wild bouts of excitement that flared up whenever he appeared. He was forever lurking in her mind, even when she was asleep. She couldn't talk about her dreams, either. If they weren't precisely *erotic,* they were certainly desire driven. She wasn't a virgin. She'd had two romances she had thought serious at the time. Both young men had been kind and funny and sexy, professional young men, good catches or so her girlfriends told her. Neither had made her feel remotely like this, and just with a *look!*

She pulled herself together, moving down the bank, rather hoping yet fearful she would go for a slide and finish up in his arms. 'This is such a beautiful place!' she said in a hushed voice.

'I knew you'd like it.' He spoke casually when he wanted to pull her into his arms and kiss that lovely soft mouth again and again. Was it his imagination or was she faintly trembling? It was hard to tell unless he *touched* her. Touched that flawless white skin that *glowed*. She was dressed simply in a ribbed tank top the same colour as her eyes and a pair of cream shorts that could never be called skimpy but nevertheless managed to draw attention to her beautiful slender legs. He never knew snowy flesh could look so good. He was used to women with tans. Even Tara who had spent a fortune on skin products had sported a golden tan.

'What did you really think of Georgy's singing?' she now asked, transferring her gaze from him to the children romping happily around the banks picking up pretty shells Dusty was busy sniffing up for them. 'You smiled but you didn't say much.'

'Here, sit down,' he said, not making the mistake of touching her but indicating a sandy ledge. He waited until she moved around him to sit down, ankles and knees together like a proper young lady. He had caught himself making mental lists of the things about her that pleased him. It was a measure of her dazzling effect on him so far he had failed to find a single thing that didn't.

'On the contrary, I distinctly remember telling Georgia how talented she is,' he pointed out, joining her on the ledge.

'Of course you *did!*' she said as though she had just remembered. 'I just had the feeling you were sort of fending off that particular talent. You wouldn't want her to be a performer when she grows up?' She tilted her head towards him, feeding on the crackling energy that was flowing her way.

Holt glanced into her eyes—quite calmly he hoped—then across the lagoon to the opposite bank where a dozen or more parrots were pillaging the bright red berries of a native bush. He had tasted them himself and found them quite tangy. 'I wouldn't be in the least surprised if she made singing her career,' he said. Why not add, after all her father is supposed to be a darn good pop singer and an excellent musician?

'That's all right then,' she said more happily. 'I thought you might have a different career in mind?'

'Did you always want to be a teacher?' he asked, shifting the questions to her.

Little yellow wild flowers their shoes had

bruised were sending up a delicious citrusy scent all around them. Now it was Marissa's turn to look away. The multicolours and the markings on the parrots were simply brilliant. 'I actually wanted to become a child psychologist. I always wanted to work with children.'

'Damaged little children?'

'Well, yes,' she said. 'I was like a doctor in waiting. I wanted to help.'

'And you *were* a damaged child. I expect that had a considerable bearing on your choosing such a profession. Why didn't you go on with it?'

Why remain a mystery to him? 'Something truly amazing happened—devastating at first—I found out I had a brother, a little half brother.'

'Keep going,' he said, giving thanks for her impulse to confide except she turned on him.

'Why do you want to know so much?' Those blue eyes flashed.

'You started it.' He didn't suppress the urge to capture her wrist, feeling the tension in her. 'Just relax. I'm your friend, not your enemy. As a matter of fact I'm your boss, but no one would ever know that. You're so astoundingly challenging I can't believe you're the governess.'

Her voice lightly shook. 'I deserved that. I'm sorry.'

'Then I forgive you, for a wonder! But I'm still waiting.'

'I don't know that I can forgive *you* for not believing me,' she retorted, with a shaky laugh. 'You've regarded Riley as my big indiscretion from day one.'

He nearly put her palm to his mouth. 'If I haven't believed you, Marissa, it's because you're to blame, in part anyway.' Slowly he released her. 'Was what happened to you so cruel you *can't* speak of it?'

She blinked her lashes rapidly, determined not to dissolve into tears. 'My father was a brilliant man, strikingly handsome. I was so proud of him. When we were all together as a family, my mother, father and me, he always said he was the happiest man in the world. He adored us, especially my mother.'

'Do you look like her?' If so her mother had to be unforgettable.

She shook her head. 'Riley and I take after our father. We have his colouring, his blue eyes. My mother was blond. After she was killed in the car crash with my father at the wheel he went to pieces. He was a man destroyed.'

'I can understand that,' he said, his own feelings solidifying into a powerful desire to keep her here with him on Wungalla.

Then she did something extraordinary. She put out her hand and lay a finger briefly against his cheek turning his face directly towards her.

'Are you *sure* you can?'

Wasn't she aware he was holding his emotions on the tightest possible rein? If the children hadn't been around he would have given into his feelings and hauled her into his arms. 'Trust me, Marissa,' he said. 'I really know what you mean. Why would you suggest otherwise? There's a hell of a lot you *don't* know about me.'

'Maybe some time you'll tell me,' she said very quietly. 'The reason I never let anyone in, is because I'm afraid they will judge him. He was a wonderful man. *Know* that. I'm certain he tried and tried, but he so *loved* her. He was desperately lonely for her. He lost all interest in life. The great wonder is he formed a relationship with Riley's mother, someone half his age. Maybe she was the one who latched on to him. That wouldn't have been totally strange. As I told you, he was a striking looking man.'

'So that was how it was?' He stared directly into her eyes, eyes what were windows opening onto her soul.

'That was how it was,' she said, letting him look his fill.

All his doubts melted away like ice under heat. 'And Riley's mother abandoned him? When did all this happen?'

Marissa picked up her story.

By the time she was finished, she was deeply upset.

Only iron discipline prevented him from lifting her right into his arms. Once he did that of course he would be damned near impossible to stop. 'You'll have to hide those tears, Marissa,' he cautioned, the warning as much for himself as her. If he had never believed there was a Fate, he believed it now. 'The children will be coming back soon.'

'Yes, I know.' She used the back of her hand to flick away fallen teardrops. 'I understand now what Catholics feel when they go to confession.'

Only he was no priest. A hard ball of tension was knotting in his stomach. 'Why don't you stop Riley from calling you Ma?'

Her blue eyes fired.

God, he wanted to grasp a handful of her hair, pull her head back.

'Because it's not as simple as that, Holt!' she declared. 'It's in the nature of every child to want a mother. Instead of being a sister I fitted into Riley's idea of a mother figure. We're very close.'

'An obvious statement,' he said harshly. 'You're going to call me Holt from now on?'

'I won't if you don't want me to. Holt just slipped out.' Why wouldn't it? That was the way she thought of him.

'No, that's okay. Just checking,' he said, his smile throwing her further off balance. 'Riley is to start calling you Marissa. You have to cut this cord. You know that. If you *don't,* you can't blame people for getting the wrong idea. Would you like me to speak to him? It might carry a little more weight coming from me. Riley and I get along well together.'

She knew that to be true. Holt McMaster was fast turning into Riley's hero figure. 'No, I'll tell him,' she said. 'Your sister-in-law.'

'My ex sister-in-law,' he corrected, tersely.

'Never even gave me a hearing. I don't under-stand that.'

'Lois didn't *want* to give you a hearing,' he said. 'Rest assured I'll make the relationship perfectly plain. Are you ashamed of your father's descent into alcoholism?'

A small silence fell. 'I don't like to say it but I must have been, if only because Aunt Allison never let up on him and his *problem.* The drinking wasn't his problem. It was a symptom. I see now part of *her* problem was the fact Uncle Bryan was secretly in love with my mother. It was her way of getting even.'

'On a *child?* How is such a thing possible?' Yet such things happened. He should know.

'She didn't really want me, you know. I was sort of forced on her.' She turned her face to him. 'Has my telling you made any difference to the way you feel about me?'

His laugh was deep and discordant. 'No!'

'I thought my being a single mother appalled you?'

'Don't be ridiculous,' he answered curtly. It wouldn't have been the way he wanted it, but he'd been fully prepared to handle it. 'I'm seriously impressed you've taken on the rearing of your half brother.' He spoke with perfect truth. 'I don't think many young women at age twenty-one would have done such a thing. You don't foresee his mother coming back into his life?'

Marissa lowered her dark glossy head with its blue-black sheen. Her hair had grown much longer than she had ever worn it, tumbling down her back. 'I told you every effort was made to find her. I think myself she probably went back to wherever she came from. She definitely didn't want Riley. I hadn't mentioned this, but she used to mistreat him.'

'Good God!' Holt groaned, thinking of the way Tara had been with Georgia. Only the odd smack, but the constant belittling of the child.

'Perhaps I'll ask you about *your* blighted marriage some time,' Marissa said, aware their relationship had progressed in huge leaps and bounds as if something in the one signalled to the other.

He trained his brilliant black eyes on her. 'That's some ask, Ms Devlin.'

'I really want to help Georgy,' she said evasively. 'I know all about loss.'

'Georgy isn't fretting about losing her mother.' His tone was abrupt, even hard. 'She is suffering loss but it's her *idea* of a mother she misses, just as Riley has substituted you. In short Tara no more wants her daughter than Riley's mother wants him. Not every woman is cut out for the maternal role it seems. Some women feel trapped. At any rate there was no future for Tara with me. None at all.'

'You sound cruel. *Are* you cruel?'

'Definitely.'

'I don't think so.' She was observing him closely.

'Don't try to analyse me, Ms Devlin,' he said, his tone giving little indication of the strength of his inner reactions.

'Because I might find it exhausting?' He was such a complex man.

'Something like that.' He shrugged his shoulders, then changed the subject. 'I haven't seen you ride yet.'

She smiled at him, seraphic and alluring at one and the same time. This was one fascinating woman.

'Why do you want to? You won't let me have a decent horse until you've checked me out?'

My God in every way! His desire for her was deepening every second he was in her company. He was even starting to *fear* it. He had no excuse. He had seen it coming. His very arms were aching from the hard restraint he was putting on them not to grab her like some damned caveman. 'That's right,' he answered, amazed his voice sounded normal when his feelings were downright primitive. 'If you can get up at dawn tomorrow morning I'll meet you down at the stables. We can go for a gallop.'

'Oh, I'd love that!' Her smile blossomed again just to haunt him. Such smiles were dangerous. They demanded he keep his defence mechanisms impossibly high.

In another minute the children laughing and puffing raced back to where they were sitting, Dusty running alongside, thoroughly enjoying his off-duty time. Georgy reached out to grasp Marissa's hand. 'Come on, you two,' she said, open affection in her voice. 'You can't sit here all day. Let's go for a walk along the bank. Riley is brilliant at nature studies. He said your dad taught him lots of things, Marissa. He must have been a wonderful man, your dad?' Georgy stared with kindly sympathy into Marissa's eyes.

'He was,' Marissa somehow managed to respond. There was a lump in her throat and unshed tears in her eyes.

Georgy jerked a head back to Riley. 'I've told *him* to stop calling you Ma,' she announced firmly. 'Marissa is an absolutely beautiful name. Ma makes it sound like you're his mother and you aren't. Keile was his mother, right?'

'I've told Georgy lots of things,' Riley explained quickly to his sister, then broke off as a large black and white bird sporting a long pink bill with a distinctive suspended pouch began to gracefully circle the lagoon before coming in to land. It tilted its large body back and spread its great wings so they acted like air brakes.

'Oh, look it's a pelican!' Riley cried, ecstatically. 'The bird that never dies!'

'Oh, but it does, Riley,' Georgy told him kindly.

'Wait until I tell you the aboriginal legend,' he said. 'I've never seen so many different species of birds in all my life. You ought to try to draw them, Georgy.'

'Oh, I will!' said Georgy, adding yet another ambition to her list.

Holt rose to his feet, lending a hand to Marissa. She took it trying to keep an impassive face at his touch, but in order to do that she had to hold her breath.

'Out of the mouths of babes!' he murmured.

'It does serve the purpose.' She smiled in relief.

In the weeks leading up to Christmas Marissa felt as though her life had caught fire. She lived in a constant state of knife-keen excitement that was bliss. At different times she even had the strange sensation she was walking on air. There was a reason of course. There always is. But only as she lay in bed in the dark did she allow herself to admit to it. She was helplessly, hopeless, deliriously in love. Fate might have brought her to Wungalla but she still had the sense to know at some time in the future it would all come to an end.

But for *now,* she couldn't accept an end was in sight.

To add to her joy, Riley thrived. Flesh covered his fragile bones. He hadn't experienced a single attack of his debilitating asthma though she always remained on alert. These days, just as

Georgy had insisted, he had dropped the *Ma* for Marissa, never once slipping back. Georgy, the one-time *enfant terrible* had turned into a cheerful fun-filled little person. A pretty child she wasn't—though gentle kindness, care and understanding were greatly benefitting her looks—but she was fast developing a personality. As an old lady she'd probably be spoken of as a 'real character.' These days she sang freely, filled with confidence and they all enjoyed hearing her.

Both children in fact were flourishing. They approached their studies with enthusiasm, vying with one another to see who could produce the best work. Riley was a very bright little boy—Marissa was proud of him—but she was secretly pleased Georgy was giving him a run for his money. Georgy was a highly intelligent little girl. All that had happened was, her abilities had been driven undercover by her own aggressive behaviour. She had been sad and lonely, questioning her own worth. But no more! The classroom was a happy place; the competition good for both children. It kept them on their toes.

To everyone's surprise and delight Catherine's fragile health went into a period of remission. She came downstairs most days showing renewed interest in everything that was going on around her. Often she allowed Marissa—sometimes with the children, sometimes not—to drive her to her favourite haunts on the station, telling fascinating stories of 'the old days' interwoven with the aboriginal legends Marissa and the children loved. It was Marissa who had Catherine's largely unused—Catherine *hated* it—but extremely efficient wheelchair brought downstairs so they could all go for a long walk late afternoon close on sunset when the air was blessedly cool and they could enjoy the glorious spectacle of a desert sunset every last one a masterpiece of crimson, bold golds and pinks. All the paths of the home gardens interlocked and Holt, enormously grateful for his grandmother's better health and outlook, and the harmony that existed, put a couple of men onto the job of clipping back any branching foliage that might impede the progress of the wheelchair.

'I think what you and I ought to do,' he said to Marissa one evening after dinner, 'is sign a lifetime contract.'

Her whole body vibrated, but she managed to keep her cool. 'Why, are you planning a large family?'

'I am toying with the idea,' he said.

Of course he would remarry. She knew that, even if the thought tortured her.

* * *

Just as the household was settling into a kind of thrilling serenity the fragile peace was broken. But there it was, *life!*

A week before Christmas Tara McMaster, *the tigress,* arrived unannounced.

'My God!' Olly exclaimed in horror, when she caught sight of the open Jeep sweeping through the eight-foot-high wrought-iron gates of the home compound and up the driveway with Tara at the wheel. 'Here comes Trouble!' A lapsed Catholic Olly blessed herself swiftly as though warding off the evil eye.

She tore through to the Garden Room where Marissa and the children were enjoying morning tea with Catherine as had become routine.

'What *is* it, Olly?' Catherine asked in alarm, taking one look at Olly's stricken face.

'It's Tara,' Olly announced in a jittery voice that didn't even sound like her own. 'She's here. She must have commandeered one of the Jeeps.'

'Dear God!' Catherine released a huge sigh of her own. 'The cheek of her after all she—' Catherine broke off, becoming aware of the children again. 'I don't believe she was invited.' Urgently she turned her gaze on Marissa. 'Go get Holt,' she urged. 'Don't go the front way. You'll have to go out back to the stables. Take one of the horses. You know where Holt is?'

'Yes, but I don't like to leave you.'

'Don't worry about me. Go *now,*' Catherine repeated, her voice firming into an order. 'We need Holt here. I can hold the fort until he arrives. You children—' she waved a finger at them '—go upstairs to the classroom. Take those little cakes with you. I trust you to behave. We'll call you when we're ready.'

'Yes, Gran,' Georgy said, all sensible obedience. Both children were already on their feet, Riley saucer-eyed, convinced something bad was going to happen.

Marissa bent quickly to kiss him. 'Go with Georgy now. I won't be long.'

'She's no business coming here!' Georgy said fiercely, taking charge of Riley's hand. 'No business at all!'

'You can say that again!' Olly muttered.

She took Nabila, a beautiful Arabian mare, so pale a grey it was almost white. Already she loved the highly intelligent and sensitive horse. She had been absolutely *thrilled* when Holt had given her permission to ride the proud yet affectionate animal. Obviously she had passed muster that first morning when he had checked out her riding ability. From that day on Nabila was put at her disposal, presumably for the duration of her term as Georgy's governess.

At first she had been concerned Nabila might have been Tara's horse, but Holt was quick to assure her Nabila had been ridden by his sisters.

'They were born in the saddle just like I was. They're careful to handle the breed properly. Gentle as Nabila is, she doesn't like a rough hand. Arabs are spirited, hot blooded creatures after all. They have great communication skills with the right rider. What I've seen this morning is enough to tell me she'll be in good hands.'

Recommendation indeed!

But the great worry was everything might come to a swift end for her and Riley with the arrival of Tara's mother. Marissa hadn't the slightest doubt Lois had filled her sister's ears with a whole lot of malicious misinformation. And Tara was a scary lady! She couldn't bear to picture her with Holt…Tara's hands on his marvellous body…the two of them making love. She had to block it out.

And what of Georgy who had been making such wonderful progress? Catherine, who was enjoying a blessed period of pain relief? Were these great benefits to be destroyed by Tara's interference?

So many questions! The answers would come soon enough.

The Arab, the creature Allah had created to 'fly without wings' took off across the flats with the speed and responsiveness Marissa had rapidly become used to. The big pre-Christmas muster had been going on for a couple of weeks now. Stock that had been allowed to wander into the Simpson Desert in search of feed had to be brought back and the clean skins hiding in the lignum swamps flushed out.

Holt spotted the charter flight coming in over Wungalla before any of the others down at the holding yards. Immediately the alarm bells rang as his mind sprang to his ex-wife. She would have returned home from her overseas trip by now, hell bent on causing trouble once she heard what poor embittered, jealous Lois had to say. Though Tara didn't care a fig for her child she would *use* Georgia any way she could.

Tara, he had learned to his cost, had little understanding of the normal codes of social and moral behaviour. To her Georgia was simply a pawn to be moved this way or that. He shot a comment to Bart his overseer about their likely visitor and got a wry smile back. Bart had been on Wungalla for over twenty years. He did a terrific job, rising from jackeroo to head stockman to trusted overseer and the most loyal of employees. There wasn't much Bart didn't know about the McMaster family's affairs but he had never lost a single mark telling tales.

There was nothing else for it but to return to the homestead. He knew a moment of violent resentment towards Tara who couldn't control Lois and their whole family. No way was he going to subject *his* family and he included the children and Marissa who he knew was the prime target and the reason for Tara's being here, to one of Tara's spiteful rages.

He hauled himself into the saddle then rode away from the mustering yard, breaking into a gallop as soon as he hit the open plain. He wished now he had driven to the site—he would have been back at the homestead quicker—but he always preferred to ride with the men.

It turned out he wasn't the only one out for a gallop. In the distance he could see a rider approaching at speed. It was Marissa on Nabila. They were coming at one hell of a pace. His sisters were fine riders, but Marissa was better. She seemed to take communication with her mount— and Nabila was a very spirited animal—to a different level. He guessed his grandmother had sent her to warn him of Tara's arrival.

Holt smiled grimly. Ever since that final outburst from Lois in Sydney he knew Tara would eventually turn up on Wungalla.

They reined in alongside, their horses acknowledging one another. 'You must come home at once.' Marissa delivered Catherine's message, adrenaline coursing through her blood. 'Your wife has arrived.'

His striking face was thunderous. 'My *ex*-wife.'

'That's right, your ex-wife.' Marissa caught her breath. 'Catherine sent me.'

Mad as he was, he almost smiled. His grandmother rarely gave anyone permission to call her by her first name, but so drawn was she to Marissa, she'd done exactly that. 'Was Tara inside the house when you left?'

She shook her head. 'No, but she'll be inside now. Catherine told me to ride out after you.'

'There's nothing to be frightened of, Marissa.' He stared directly into her eyes. She was wearing a cream akubra and her beautiful hair showed all around her face and rippled down her back. 'I'll listen to what she has to say, then I'll tell her to go right back home again. She's not welcome on Wungalla. She knows that.'

'Everything was going so well!' Marissa lamented. 'Do you think she wants to take Georgy away?'

Holt clicked his tongue in disgust. 'That's the *last* thing she'll want to do. Tara can't live on her settlement forever even if I was far too generous. She'll be looking for another rich husband.' Most men wouldn't want to rear another man's child.

The conviction in his tone had the effect of calming her. 'Catherine is distressed,' she said, distressed herself. 'Georgy on the other hand is furious but remarkably obedient. She did exactly what she was told.'

'Good!' His eyes moved to the rapid rise and fall of her breasts. 'Take your time coming back.'

She shook her head. 'I'll come with you. Nabila has plenty of stamina.'

'Right then, let's ride!'

CHAPTER SEVEN

HOLT strode into the entrance hall—no back way for him—having told Marissa to go upstairs and stay out of the way. But Tara was stunningly quick. All the while she and Catherine had been attempting conversation, her ears had been trained to the slightest footfall. No one, least of all her, could mistake Holt's tread. It just rang with authority.

She leapt up from her chair 'Please excuse me, Catherine, but I do believe the Master of Wungalla has returned!'

Catherine at the end of her tether drew a deep sigh of relief.

Tara made a rush for the entrance hall, conscious of the thrills that were running up and down her spine. It was the sorriest day of her life she and Holt had been divorced. 'Holt, *darling!*' she cried effusively, throwing up ultraslim arms. 'Surprise, surprise!'

'On the other hand no surprise at all,' he said, evading the kiss that came to rest on his chin.

'Well, I never could do the right thing with you, could I, my darling! Ah, there you are, Ms Devlin!' Tara swung her elegant blond head away from Holt just in time to see Marissa set foot on the first landing. 'Please, do come down again. You'd think being Georgia's mother I'd want a word. Holt darling, aren't you going to introduce us? Ms Devlin is my daughter's governess is she not? Naturally I'm interested in meeting her.' She laughed as though she'd just made a joke.

'Go on upstairs, Marissa,' Holt gave her a piercing look.

'Ah, the man who is always obeyed' Tara crowed 'If you want to be difficult about this, darling, let's be difficult. But I'd like to meet Ms Devlin *now!'*

Holt's expression would have given anyone pause. 'Either you behave, Tara, or risk being bundled off Wungalla.'

'Now isn't that just typical of you!' Tara cried, managing to break off as Catherine made slow halting progress into the entrance hall.

Yet Catherine's voice was very clear and firm. 'You really should have considered a career on the stage, Tara,' she said. 'Being able to act out your feelings might have saved you.'

'*Saved* me! You do make me sound a sorry plight. But then you never did like me did you?'

An expression of extreme bitterness crossed her sharp featured, arresting face.

'I certainly *tried,*' Catherine said, her own face a mask.

'May I help you upstairs, Mrs McMaster?' Marissa intervened, coming back down the stairs again. Catherine's voice may have sounded normal, but she had suddenly reverted to looking as fragile as a bird.

'I'd appreciate that, Marissa,' Catherine said.

Holt raised his hand. 'It's okay, Marissa. I'll take you, Gran. Go along to the study, Tara. I'll join you there in a few minutes.'

'But of course, darling!' Tara nodded, all co-operation. 'Good idea! Miss Devlin can keep me company until you return. Marissa, is it? What a pretty name!'

'It just so happens I want Marissa to look in on the children,' Holt said, getting a protective arm around his grandmother.

Marissa felt herself torn two ways. She had no wish to run and hide from Tara, but it *was* her job to respect Holt's wishes. Tara settled it by grabbing her arm, her grip amazingly strong for a woman pared down to the bone. But then Tara was probably as frail as a bulldozer, Marissa thought. 'Ms Devlin can spare a few moments,

Holt. You're such a hard man. Isn't he a hard man?' Bizarrely she appealed to Marissa.

Holt's handsome face registered a variety of emotions, disgust uppermost. 'I'll be back in a moment, Marissa,' he said shortly, gathering up Catherine who looked as if the stresses and strains of having Tara back in the house again had caught up with her.

'Come along now, Ms Devlin,' Tara said, suddenly looking at Marissa with she had to interpret as outright hatred.

'Certainly, but please let go of my arm.' Marissa reminded herself she had nothing to fear. 'I'm quite happy to talk to you about your daughter, Mrs McMaster. Georgy is a remarkable little girl.'

Tara shot her a look of malicious contempt. 'Oh, for God's sake, don't try to butter me up. There's *nothing* remarkable about Georgia, except her lack of looks and lack of intelligence.'

Marissa felt chilled to the bone. 'I'm saddened you think that way. Georgy is highly intelligent. I would say a gifted child. As for her looks? Now I've met you, Mrs McMaster, I can see a resemblance.' She wasn't just saying that to provoke Tara. She *could*. Georgy as an adult would have similar sharp features. Tara was very elegant, very glamorous, but she was no natural beauty. She was a woman who had made the absolute most of herself.

'Clearly you've got poor eyesight,' Tara said acidly. 'You can't imagine what it was like for me producing such a child! She was the ugliest baby I think I've ever seen. It was shocking for me. No wonder I rejected her.'

'Maybe you weren't functioning properly, Mrs McMaster,' Marissa suggested. 'You may have been suffering from postnatal depression?'

Tara nodded sharply. 'Probably. I was desperately upset. It was the start of all our problems. I blame Georgia for the breakup of our marriage. I know Holt secretly despises her.'

Marissa's shock translated into anger and dismay. 'That's appalling and simply not true.'

'Show's what you know!' Tara mocked. 'Holt's no closer to her than I am.' She caught Marissa's arm again. 'Tell me. Don't you think a man like Holt McMaster would be bitterly, *bitterly,* disappointed in a mentally defective child?'

Marissa broke away, moving swiftly ahead to open the door of Holt's study. 'You shock me, Mrs McMaster. Really you do. And you couldn't be more wrong.' She stood back so Tara could enter the book and trophy filled room. 'Georgy's behavioural problems, her temper tantrums and so forth, arose out of a deep unhappiness.'

Tara flounced into a leather armchair, her rejection of Marissa and her ideas abundantly apparent. 'She was like a little wild animal, scratching, biting, always screaming at me, "I hate you!" I was left with no choice. Who gives up their daughter anyway unless they're driven into it? Holt turned away from me. He became a different person. We'd been *sooo* happy before Georgia arrived.'

Marissa was startled into saying, 'Really?'

'Yes, of course really. You wouldn't know the first thing about my marriage.'

Except it wasn't made in Heaven! 'Why are you here, Mrs McMaster?' Marissa asked, very quietly. She was eyeing Tara steadily, adding up all her impressions.

Tara's blond head shot up, a vertical line between her delicately arched brows. 'I hardly see how that's any of *your* business?' The outrage in her voice and expression brought back memories of her sister, Lois, although Lois was only a shadow of her older sibling.

'It is in this way,' Marissa said reasonably. 'Georgy has taken great steps forward. These days she's a happy, contented co-operative child, a pleasure to teach.'

Tara obviously couldn't conceive of that. 'I find that *very* difficult to believe, Ms Devlin,' she said. 'Georgia never did act like a normal child. Why? Because she's *not* normal.'

Marissa studied the other woman, horribly mesmerised. 'Did you ever question whether she was getting a *normal* upbringing? Your own unhappiness may have been a cause. If you insist on thinking of Georgy as mentally defective, which is really preposterous, is it so surprising she felt rejected and emotionally deprived?'

'Excuse me!'

For a fraction of a second Marissa thought Tara was about to jump up and attack her.

'Who are *you* to attempt to psychoanalyse *me?*' Tara demanded to know. 'You who have made a total mess of *your* life.'

'But you know nothing about my life,' Marissa said. 'Neither does your sister.'

'What are you here for, Tara?' Holt suddenly appeared behind Marissa, looking and sounding totally exasperated. He closed the study door. 'What the real reason you've come?'

'Why to see my daughter.' Tara opened her green eyes wide. 'And I have to admit check out what sort of person you've hired as a governess. Lois told me she has a child in tow. Single mother is that it, dear?' She addressed Marissa. 'You must have fallen pregnant very young? I'm worldly enough to understand it.'

'But you don't understand it, Mrs McMaster,' Marissa said, just beating the taut faced Holt to an answer. 'Riley is my *brother,* my half brother. We share the same father. Your sister got it wrong, as well.'

Tara's face froze ludicrously, as though she was totally unused to being contradicted by anyone. 'Well, just let me say this, Ms Devlin. You're being thoroughly checked out as we speak.' She lifted her head to Holt. 'I *know* these girls, Holt. But this one is pretty with a Capital P. Makes a difference, doesn't it?'

'Let's go back to pretty and substitute *exquisite,*' Holt said, turning his brilliant dark gaze on Marissa. 'You can go now, Marissa.'

'Yes, dear, go on upstairs,' Tara chimed in, waving a dismissive hand. 'We don't need you any more. I've *seen* exquisite little you. Holt is a sucker for beauty. I was sort of hoping Lois was exaggerating but there you are!'

Holt waited a few moments before he took a seat behind the massive partner's desk. 'All right, Tara. What is it?'

She gave him what she hoped was a seductive smile, feeling true despair and anger herself for having lost him. 'I wanted to see you. Is that so difficult to believe?'

'Actually, yes,' he said. 'I didn't think you capable of much feeling at all.'

'Then you're out of your brain. I love you, Holt. When you loved me was the most wonderful time of my life.'

'Except I never loved *you,* Tara. The Tara you pretended to be before we were married was a complete phoney. Your family wanted a carer for you. You wanted a nice meal ticket.'

'Why are you so hard,' she cried. 'You draw blood.' She sat back and narrowed her eyes at him. 'Have you got her into your bed yet? Though she doesn't exactly look *easy* to seduce. The unwanted pregnancy I expect.'

Holt exhaled. 'You're the one with the behavioural problems, Tara.'

She stared at him. Those black eyes! That beautiful, sexy mouth! 'You've condemned me for a sinner. Do you ever imagine what it might be like for us to get back together again?'

His laugh disconcerted her. 'I did it once. I'd *never* do it again. No, Tara, I don't. Why are you here? You know there isn't the remotest possibility of our kissing and making up.'

Tara had a moment of genuine grief. 'You're the best kisser I ever knew. No one can compare with you as a lover.'

'And you're someone who would really know. I don't want you upsetting Georgy, Tara.'

She shrugged. 'It was always the other way around. She upsets *me!*'

'Lois told you about Marissa, didn't she? That's why you've materialised.'

Tara gave a discordant laugh. 'You make me sound like a spook. Well, of course, Lois told me. She *had* to. She's my sister, after all, and she's no fool. She spotted the attraction right off. And you *are* attracted to her, aren't you? Women have an antennae for such things. She's not the usual little run-of-the-mill governess is she?'

'No, she's not.' Holt's tone was very firm. 'She's a miracle worker. Georgy is a different child. It's a peaceful household these days, Tara. I get down on my knees every night and thank the good Lord for it.'

'That I'd like to see, you on your knees,' she murmured, her eyes as green as grass. 'You drop-dead, sexy you!'

'Give me a break!' Holt groaned, unable to give

her the slightest response. 'Marissa's little brother, Riley, is a great kid. Like Marissa, he's had a most beneficial effect on Georgy. They're great friends.'

'So what happened to Zoltan?' Tara asked, just barely controlling her contempt. 'The way she used to talk to her imaginary friend was just *too* weird.'

'Strange, when you think you're *exceptionally* weird. I'm not going to prevent you from seeing your daughter, Tara. On the condition you try your hardest to be pleasant. I realise loving or caring is way too tough for you. When is it you plan on going back, by the way? There's no place for you here, Tara. We had that out long ago.'

Anger surged through Tara, spilling out her mouth. 'You've allowed poor stupid Lois to come. Did you know she goes to pieces every time she looks at you? She's mad for you, always was.'

'I've tried not to let it get me down,' Holt said, his expression sardonic. 'Anyway I told her the last time I saw her it's a total waste of time day-dreaming we'd somehow hook up. She has to turn her attentions elsewhere. I'm pretty sure I convinced her.'

'Oh, you did!' Tara crowed, her face lighting up with vindictiveness. 'Obviously you've decided the governess is a lot more fun.' She stood up, flicking at the creases in her impeccably cut linen slacks. 'Now do you think I could possibly see my child. I suppose she'll still remind me of my wild one-night stand.'

'Just one of hundreds more.' Holt said, getting to his feet.

'Not a one of them to match you.' Tara walked to the door. 'I've been hearing from the beauteous and blessed Ms Devlin Georgia is highly intelligent. Here I was thinking all this time she had the brain of a pea.'

Holt held the door for her. 'Well, we all know you've no expert on children.'

Marissa found the children huddled together in the classroom.

'What does she want?' Georgy asked, displaying the utmost animosity.

Marissa pulled out a chair, then sat down. 'Keep your cool, Georgy. No need to get upset. Your mother just wants to say hello.'

'No!' Georgy rejected that out of hand. 'She's come to make trouble. She's still in love with Holt, you know.'

'You mean your dad.' Riley, who had kept faithfully to calling his sister Marissa not Ma, was of the firm opinion Georgy should call her father Dad.

Georgy stood correction. 'Okay, she's still in love with Dad.'

Who could blame her!

'No way has she come to see me. I could be a joey in the pouch for all she cares about me. Did you know joeys were tiny, tiny, little things this big?' she broke off to ask Riley.

'Yes, I did.' Riley, extremely worried turned back to his sister. 'Does she know about *me*, Marissa?'

'Yes, Riley. There's no need for you to worry, either. *Please,* both of you, relax.' There was no question the children were het up, possibly fearing separation.

Georgy gave Marissa a significant, unnervingly adult look. 'You can bet your life Aunt Lois went home and told her she better get out here.'

'What *for?*' Riley asked, looking from one to the other for the reason.

'You wouldn't understand,' Georgy said, patting his hand.

'Come on, give us a clue.'

'My lips are sealed.' Georgy made a zipping motion with her hand.

A moment later Tara made her appearance, knocking on the door of the classroom. 'Where's my girl?' she carolled, her voice flowing like honey.

Georgy swivelled her head around. 'She's nowhere around here,' she replied, very rudely.

'Are you sure about that?' Tara was minded to be playful, advancing into the room and holding out her arms.

'Absolutely certain.' Georgy looked like she might explode at any minute.

Tara's laugh was like a shower of broken glass. 'You funny little thing! Come give your mother a hug.'

Holt intervened. 'She doesn't have to hug you if she doesn't want to, Tara. But you might stand up and say hello, Georgy. There are innumerable things in life we have to do when we don't want to.'

'Sure, Dad.' Georgy stood bolt upright studying her mother with hostile eyes.

Inexplicably Tara burst into another peal of laughter.

'What's the joke?' Georgy was fast falling back into the old belligerence.

'Don't be rude, dear,' Tara said, transferring her green gaze to Riley. 'Who's your little friend? Such a pretty boy! I'm so glad that monster Zoltan has vanished.'

'*You're* the monster,' Georgy shouted, pulling at her flyaway hair with an agitated hand. 'You're a real…'

'No, no, Georgy!' Marissa warned. Georgy had a vocabulary of swear words forbidden to Riley and herself for that matter. The mystery was, from where had she learned them?

Georgy's face flushed with anger but she swallowed whatever choice word she was about to unleash. 'And leave Riley alone,' she ordered her mother. 'He doesn't want to know you.'

'This isn't working, Tara,' Holt said with unconcealed grimness. 'Did you really think it would?'

Tara's expression turned serious and sorry. She shook her head. 'Obviously Georgia still needs help,' she said, with a frown. 'Ms Devlin assured me she'd turned into a model child, but it seems to me the slightest thing can set her off. It's just like the old days.'

Marissa felt driven to defending her charge. 'You're provoking her, Mrs McMaster.'

'Don't patronise me.' Tara turned on Marissa sharply. 'My daughter seems no better to me. I think it's high time I started to look for professional help for her. In fact I should take her home with me.'

It was a moment of extreme gravity when time seemed to stand still. Then Holt crossed to where Georgy was standing, taking her hand in his own. 'That sounds fine to me, Tara,' he said in a calm, accommodating voice. It astounded Marissa who hadn't thought it possible he could agree to such a thing. 'Take her by all means,' he continued in exactly the same tone of voice. 'Why not this afternoon? I can arrange it. Ms Devlin can pack Georgy's clothes in no time. Why don't you do it now, Ms Devlin.' He looked over to where Marissa was standing, his brilliant gaze quite unreadable.

Marissa was stunned. This man who had invaded her heart was no more a good father than Tara was a good mother. Hadn't Tara already said so? And I *love* him! My God! The hurt was appalling. She felt real despair. 'I'm sorry I can't do that,' she said, and her clear voice rang out. She knew full well what her refusal would mean, but she was quite prepared to be expelled. 'I care about Georgy too much. It's perfectly obvious she doesn't want to go with her mother.'

Or did she? Shaken, Marissa focused her gaze on the little girl. Pint-size Georgy appeared to have a better grip on herself than she did. Georgy was standing quietly, in her floral dress, hand in hand with a father who was about to pass her over to the mother who had abandoned her. Was she too frightened or too numb to speak? The truly perplexing thing was she looked neither.

Perhaps I'm a complete fool? Perhaps I've totally misread the situation? What do I know about marriage anyway? 'I think if I pack for anyone it will be for myself and Riley,' Marissa said, feeling slashed to the heart. 'Get up, Riley.' She held out her hand to him.

'It's okay, Riley!' Georgy gave a beseeching little cry as Riley stumbled to his feet. *'Really!'*

'Go with your sister, Riley,' Holt said, quiet but firm; an authority figure.

'Yes, sir.'

Marissa said nothing. She waited until Riley reached her, then she took him by the hand and walked out of the classroom. She wouldn't be needed here anyway. Wasn't it well within her experience dreams had a way of turning into nightmares? She had lived through quite a few. A broken heart wouldn't kill her. It hadn't in the past. She'd survive. The crucial thing to remember was in order to survive she couldn't afford to let dangerous elements into her life. She had to keep herself and Riley safe. The picture she had carried in her heart of Holt McMaster didn't faithfully portray the man. Their hero figure was fatally flawed.

Marissa spent the next hour packing, while Riley lay on the bed halfheartedly reading a book he would normally have enjoyed. From time to time he asked Marissa a question, sighing at the answer.

'I can't understand it,' he said morosely. 'Georgy told me she never wanted to see her mother again. She really meant it, too. Now she seems okay about going back to Sydney with her. I don't get it!'

'Neither do I, but life is full of surprises, Riley. Don't you worry. I'll think of something.'

'So we're really leaving?' The hope that was fading from his eyes tore at Marissa's heart.

'Well, Georgy's going. She won't need a governess any more. Her mother will probably send her to boarding school.'

'But old Mrs McMaster loves you to read to her,' Riley insisted. 'She told me. She'll still want you, won't she?'

Marissa shook her head. 'I don't think so, Riley. Don't fret. We'll be all right.'

'I really *love* it here,' he said wistfully. 'I thought we might be able to stay forever! Georgy told me she never wanted us to go. Now she's off with her mother.'

'Mothers are very important people in our lives, Riley.'

'So how come my mother took off?'

She stopped what she was doing to look at him. How dear he had become to her! His glossy curls, so much like hers, haloed his face. 'She never learned responsibility. She might have had a hard childhood herself. I'm very sad for you, Riley.'

'Don't be,' he said, giving her a heartbreaking smile. 'I have *you*. I thought Georgy was my friend. She's only tiny but she's full of fun. I'll really miss her.'

'Me, too!'

'What I *really* don't understand is why Mr McMaster is just sending Georgy off. He *knows* Georgy's mother is horrible to her.'

'Maybe *he* doesn't want her any more?' Marissa said from the depths of her misery.

'I don't believe that,' Riley said. He closed his book and sat up straight as a knock came at the door.

Marissa went to it, thinking it would be Olly. Even with the door firmly shut she had been aware of a lot of activity in the house. It would have been Olly who had the job of packing Georgy's clothes.

Her heart flipped. It was Holt. So handsome, so powerful, so daunting. A man to be worshipped. But how *could* she when he didn't know what love was?

Disconcertingly he ignored her as though she weren't there, speaking directly to Riley. 'Hop up, Riley, there's a good man. Georgy is down the hallway in her old bedroom. Olly is with her. I want you to go join them. I need to have a few words with your sister.'

'If you're mad at Marissa I'm going to stay,' Riley spoke up bravely.

'Not this time, Riley,' Holt said firmly. 'Have no fear. Go along now.'

'Yes, sir.' This time Riley didn't hesitate. 'Is Georgy *really* going with her mother?' he asked at the door.

'Her mother believes so. It's given her a very serious jolting. She didn't think for a moment I'd give my permission.'

'Neither did I!' said Marissa and a tear fell down her cheek.

'You know what *I* think,' Riley announced, staring up at Holt.

'Tell Georgy about it,' Holt said kindly, placing his hand on Riley's shoulder and ushered him out the door. He then locked it to Marissa's further shock.

By the time he turned back to her she was working very hard to hide her deep distress.

'You're leaving?' he asked, exactly like a man ready to call her a cab.

'Of course I'm leaving,' she retorted, breathing hard. 'There's no place for me here now.'

'Shouldn't *I* be the one to decide that?' he asked, his manner implying she had no say at all.

'How could you? How *could* you?' She couldn't resist the urge to go out on the attack. She stopped folding a T-shirt of Riley's to round on him, condemnation blazing out of her blue eyes. 'I can't believe you'd hand Georgy over like that!'

He sat down on the end of her bed, as if he had no intention of getting up any time soon. 'You're going to dig yourself into a bigger hole if you don't stop now,' he cautioned.

She turned her eyes away, refusing to be intimidated. 'I'm *not* going to say I'm sorry.' She resumed what she was doing, her normally competent hands badly shaking. She was coming far too close to betraying herself.

'How do you propose to get out of here?' he asked, studying her so intently he mightn't have seen her for years.

'The same way I got in,' she answered shortly, battling the uncontrollable rush of excitement whenever he was near.

'I flew you in as I recall.'

'I'd forgotten, but you know what I mean. I can drive out.'

'To where?'

'Oh, hell, I don't know *exactly* where!' She spoke furiously, goaded by the arrogance of his manner. 'But it won't be your business anymore.' Her hair was cascading all around her flushed face so she stalked away to the dressing table to find an elastic band. One was to hand so she wound her hair into a loose ponytail.

'And the clothes in the wardrobe?' He indicated a number of items that were hanging in the tall open armoire. 'Are you leaving them as mementoes of your stay?'

She closed her eyes, trying to gather her wildly fragmented thoughts. 'They're Fran's. Olly very kindly lent them to me until my things arrived.'

'I thought I'd seen that silver thing before,' he remarked. 'You're feeling very unhappy aren't you?'

'Aren't *you?*' She shook her head in wonder.

'You blame me totally?'

'How could I even begin to explain?' She was afraid she was going to burst into tears. 'You're top of my list of lousy fathers.'

Immediately she said it her whole body tensed up. Instant dismissal was definitely in sight.

'Now haven't *you* got a cheek?' he murmured, very softly.

Soft or not it would have given anyone pause. But a wild light flashed in Marissa's eyes. 'I thought you were so *different*, Holt! It's too tremendously, shockingly, *awful*, for you to turn into someone else.'

His handsome mouth twisted. 'You sound like you're a little in love with me?'

Shock slammed into her. 'Don't be ridiculous!'

she protested, knowing she wasn't doing a good enough job of it. They were barely a foot apart, close enough for him to touch her, but he didn't.

'I'm not sure that's true.' He rose to his much superior height. 'Look at me.'

'I will *not!*' She jerked away, painfully aware that the ache of excitement had taken over her body.

'I only want to see if you're telling the truth.'

Hardly aware she was doing it she continued to back away until apparently he'd had enough of it. Clamping his strong hands under her armpits, as one might a naughty child, he backed her up against the wall. 'You really need a good tongue lashing, but a kiss will have to do.'

She couldn't seem to breathe, let alone *think.* She stared up at him, intensely emotional, head spinning, primitive emotions smashing through all her defences; her pride and self-esteem. He had disappointed her bitterly, betrayed Georgy. Even then she wanted him with every fibre of her being. Her very will was crashing. 'No, wait!' Conscience prodded her into making a final attempt to salvage something. 'Holt, *wait!*'

He simply took her face between his hands. 'I think I've waited long enough. Why can't you *trust* me?' He spoke very sombrely, a dark brooding in his eyes.

She stared at him now, as though trying to see through to his soul. Except all she saw was a reflection of herself in the brilliance of his eyes. 'I did. I thought I did.' She struggled not to cry. 'But I never…'

'Because of Georgy?' he asked, one hand moving to encircle her throat.

Her first instinct was to rest her cheek against his hand. Impossible! Yet there was a mad urgency in her. He had induced it as if he had thrown a switch. Sensations crackled and flared. She felt them in her breasts, in her blood, in the apex of her body, quivering beneath the thrusts of sexual desire. Her whole being *mocked* her. Mocked the high-minded position she had taken. Then she realised, for the very first time ever, the tremendous power of passion.

'I *told* you,' she muttered, trying to angle her head away, at the same time ravished by his touch. 'I wish more than anything…'

She got no further. With a sound like a soft growl, his mouth came down over hers, hard, punishing but so incredibly voluptuous she would have fallen to the floor if he hadn't been holding her up. Desire bubbled up like hot lava, spilling through her veins and carrying all before it with frightening speed. *Nothing* could equal this! No sliver of resistance had even entered her mind. Instead she was holding on to him for dear life. It was all she *could* do when he had such power over her. What she had wished for so ardently, what she had dreamed so vividly was really happening. She knew it wasn't right, but she couldn't stop it. She didn't *want* to.

Heart pounding she let him open her mouth fully to his avid exploration. She didn't really know what he thought of her, but she did know *one* thing. He *wanted* her. Her body was crushed against him so she could feel his powerful arousal. Their tongues circled…mated. His hands moved down to her breasts as though he had read her mind, shaping them over the little tank top she wore, his thumbs working the highly sensitive nipples.

She was breathing him in, murmuring his name, yielding when she should be fighting, letting him half drag half carry her towards the bed. Somehow this tremendous *need* had to be assuaged. Some flicker of awareness entered her brain. This man of iron control had lost it. She couldn't help him. She had lost it, too. It was like a spell had been placed on them; one that denied them the capacity for rational thought.

God, what am I doing? Jaw clenched with the effort Holt fought hard to find focus. He was travelling straight down the path he swore he wouldn't. This beautiful, intelligent young woman was under his protection yet he was ravenous to peel off all her clothes and make love to her; ravenous to push them both to the limit. She wasn't helping, reacting to him with such control shattering intensity it took everything he had to bring their headlong rush to have sex to an abrupt end.

Using his considerable strength, he tossed her onto the big, springy bed watching her supple body bounce on impact. A feeble little cry broke from her throat. Then she righted herself, pushing herself up on one elbow, to speak to him. Her small breasts were heaving, her hair tumbling wildly all around her lovely face, her porcelain skin flushed like a rose.

Marissa shoved back her hair, trying to get her breath under control. 'Oh, God, Holt! How can I stay here after *that?*'

A shadow of anger crossed his face; hard anger at himself. Yet he spoke harshly. 'Don't act so surprised. It's a place we were coming to.'

Of course it was. Her eyes glittered with the knowledge but it didn't prevent her from springing off the bed, going towards him, temper up. 'So you saw that from the beginning, did you?' She was stung by such arrogance.

'That's right. So did you,' he told her, unimpressed.

She nearly choked on the words. 'Speak for yourself, Holt McMaster!'

He let out an infuriating shout of laughter that held little humour. 'And you leading me on every single day?'

She fell back automatically, heat sizzling her skin. 'You're accusing *me* of leading *you* on?' she asked incredulously.

His answer couldn't have been more blunt. 'Yes.'

Nothing made sense. He wanted this to stop. He wanted it to intensify. Eyes brilliant with frustration, he hauled her back to him, one arm curling around her body, acutely aware the flames of desire were still burning fiercely. Yet he showed none of it in his voice. 'If it's at *all* possible, I'd like you to stay quiet for the rest of the day. That means stay in this room. Stay out of the way.' It was an order.

She wanted to rage at him but she was trembling too much. She could no more smother the flames that burned in her than he could. The only difference was *she* was showing it. 'But that's crazy! Are you going to *lock* me in?'

His grip tightened. He was on fire! in his belly, in his loins, in his skin. 'I will if I'm pushed,' he threatened, his eyes pitch-black. 'You can fill in the time unpacking. You're not going anywhere.'

She couldn't read him at all. She felt contempt for herself, at the same time she was nearly jumping out of her skin. It was all too shockingly perverse! 'Are you saying you're going to think of something *else* for me to do?' she asked with extreme sarcasm. Might as well! She had already burned her boats.

His gaze locked on hers. 'I already have.'

It was as though he had forged a brand on her. 'Then I decline.' She threw up her chin but all she got was a tight smile.

'Crossing me isn't something you should do lightly. We had a contract of sorts.'

'You were the one who broke it!' she retorted on the instant.

'And here I was thinking you could read me better than that!' He released her so suddenly she staggered, clutching at a chair.

'Why are you making me feel so confused?' she asked, her voice shot through with bewilderment.

He shrugged his wide shoulders, then turned away as though he had much more important things to do than come up with an answer. 'You'll have to work that out for yourself.'

'Wait!' She couldn't afford not to make one last try for Georgy's sake. She covered the distance between them, making a grab for his arm before he reached the door. 'Holt, please don't send Georgy away. *Please,* I beg of you!' She stared up at him with passionate blue eyes, bright as jewels.

'What would you do to prevent it?'

He asked it in such a way she gasped. He meant *sleep* with him, of course. What a heaven that would be! What a hell!

She continued to stare at him, scared of herself as much as him. 'What is it you *mean?*' Her voice was scarcely above a whisper.

He laughed then, a wry sound. 'I want you to allow *me* to handle this, Ms Devlin,' he said turning away.

There was nothing to do but hold up her hands in acknowledgement.

CHAPTER EIGHT

TARA stormed into her daughter's bedroom, demanding to know exactly what was going on. It didn't make a lot of sense to Olly. Tara already knew she had been instructed to pack Georgy's things.

Olly shrugged, then pushed herself out of the big comfortable armchair, straightening her spine. She had been expecting Tara's disagreeable appearance for close on an hour. Holt had taken the Jeep down to the airstrip to make his checks on the Beech Baron. He wasn't losing any time getting his ex-wife off the station. Meanwhile she had to hold the fort. Holt had given his orders. Under no condition was his grandmother to be disturbed. Marissa was to be confined to her room along the corridor. Olly understood perfectly Marissa's presence on Wungalla was to Tara just as it had been to her sister, Lois, like a red flag to a bull. Marissa's beauty, intelligence and refinement had totally panicked them, offering the very first *real* threat since the divorce.

'And what's all that?' Tara snorted, pointing a furious finger at two pieces of luggage standing near the door.

'Why it's Georgy's things!' Olly explained in apparent amazement. She looked at the luggage, then back at Tara. 'Mr McMaster asked me to pack them, remember? Aren't you taking her back to Sydney?'

'You *said* you were!' Georgy lifted her head accusingly. She and Riley had been poring over a game of Chinese Checkers now she broke off, giving every appearance of a child who had set her heart on going with her mother.

Tara stood rigid for a moment without responding. 'Where's Holt?' she cried, shooting another piercing glance at Olly.

'Why he's gone to check on the plane,' Olly was good at feigning surprise. 'Naturally he wants to fly you out himself.'

'Today?' Tara laughed like the idea was absolutely preposterous.

All three stared back at her, blank faced. Everything was in readiness.

'Where's the governess?' Tara asked, her voice rising on a note of hysteria.

Used to Tara's mood swings, Olly jumped. 'No doubt the girl's packing,' she said. 'There'll be nothing for her to do now you're taking Georgy back with you.'

'Am I?' Tara shook her head, then she suddenly picked up one of the children's books lying on the bed and threw it hitting the French doors. 'I want to see her,' she said. 'I want to make absolutely sure of that.' She turned to the door but to her astonishment the children raced past her, blocking her way. *'I beg your pardon!'* she shrieked, her nostrils quivering. 'Are you totally out of your mind?'

'Absolutely!' said Georgy, never given to half measures. 'Dad said you weren't to bother Marissa.' She spoke stoutly, but she was swallowing nevertheless. Her mother did look scary with her face all bunched up like that.

'Dad!' For an instant Tara looked like a snake about to strike. *'Dad!'* she repeated, spitting out the word with the utmost contempt. 'The two of you better get out of my way.'

Olly always slow to temper came straight to the boil. 'Don't you *dare* touch a hair of their heads,' she said, coming to range herself alongside the children.

Tara gave the housekeeper the coldest stare. 'Why, you stupid, insolent creature!' she gasped. 'Have you gone mad, as well?' She wheeled out an arm and thrust the featherweight Riley out of the way. 'If it were up to me you'd be sacked in a minute. You never did know your place.'

'You, neither!' said Olly, looking unrepentant.

But Tara was already out in the hallway making a lightning quick dash for the west wing. This simply wasn't happening, she told herself. The very last thing she wanted was custody of her pesky little daughter. Taking her back to Sydney for maybe a week max was just a plot to get rid of the governess. Holt could get another one in the New Year. Preferably one who looked like a camel.

Inside her bedroom Marissa heard the procession coming her way. Her nerves were stretched to their fullest extent. Had Tara changed her mind or had Holt taken a different stance? She prayed that was so, starting to see it as some sort of strategy Holt had worked out. If so, her outspokenness, and her lack of trust in him were really unforgivable even if her heart was in the right place.

Tara didn't bother with the niceties. She barged in the unlocked door, followed up by Olly and the children.

'Doesn't anyone bother about knocking any more?' Marissa asked mildly enough.

Georgy stepped around Olly and took control. 'We told her not to come. Dad said you weren't to be disturbed.'

'Just forget *Dad!*' Tara snarled, thrusting her daughter aside. 'This insolent woman—' she gestured threateningly towards Olly '—told me you were packing to leave. I see no luggage!' She twisted around to face the armoire, pulling open one of the doors to reveal a rack of clothes.

'Those things belong to Holt's sister, Fran,' Marissa explained quickly. 'Olly very kindly lent them to me as I had to wait on most of my own things arriving. What is it you want, Mrs McMaster?'

'I want to make sure you're being shown the door,' Tara said, not bothering to repress her dislike and distaste.

'That's hardly your business,' Marissa said. Trying to placate Tara would get her absolutely nowhere anyway. 'I *will* be leaving however. As you're taking Georgy back to Sydney, I no longer have a job.'

Georgy cleared her throat noisily, looking at her mother with wide eyes. 'That's *right!*'

Riley on the other hand appeared to be struck dumb.

'You *are* taking her?' Marissa sought confirmation, not being able to find it in Tara's bizarre manner.

'Of course she's taking her!' Holt's voice startled them all. For a big man he hadn't made a sound on his approach. He strode into the room looking towards his ex-wife. 'Everything's set. We can leave within the hour.'

Tara looked back with burning eyes. Then she threw up her hands with manic energy, seizing on a lovely little Lladro sculpture of a ballerina, then smashing it with all her might.

'Wonderful!' Holt shook his head as though such an act of barbarism wasn't entirely unexpected, but Georgy, standing quietly one minute, the very next was across the room pummelling into her mother.

'You're the most disgusting person I've ever met,' she yelled.

Tara's sharp good-looking face contorted with rage and shock. 'You wicked little girl!' She lifted a hand to retaliate, only Holt's voice cracked like thunder.

'*Stop!* Both of you. You know, you're absolutely right, Tara,' he said grimly, tension tightening the strong planes of his face. 'Georgy does need counselling. I can't pretend I'm not extremely sad to lose her but I have to admit we can't manage. I just hope you're going to be generous enough to allow me to see Georgy whenever I want.'

Tara's face unclenched. She gave him such an *odd* smile. 'But I don't want her to *live* with me permanently, Holt. You know that. She's much better off here. All I want is to take her back to Sydney where she can get proper attention from a child psychologist.'

'Tara, what sort of a solution is that?' he asked reasonably. 'I'm certain any child psychologist would recommend your daughter stay with *you*. That's how I see it anyway. You take Georgy today, you take her until she no longer needs you. Probably when she's ready to go to university. You've taken a stand. That's mine. Georgy.' He turned back to the child. 'You remember what I told you?'

'Sure, Dad.' Georgy looked at the floor.

'Yes, yes, *Dad!*' Tara gave another one of those weird laughs.

'Well, we'd better make a start,' Holt said. 'I really appreciate your trying, Tara, at long last.' He picked up the two suitcases. 'We'll go downstairs, while Georgy says her goodbyes.' The dazed Tara allowed herself to be shepherded before him and out of the room.

For long moments nobody moved. Then at last, Marissa asked, 'What's going on, Georgy?' Her mind was in chaos. She was looking for answers but so far couldn't find them.

'Shh!' Georgy held a finger against her lips.

'Georgy this is *serious!*' Riley whispered conspiratorially. 'Tell Marissa, now!'

'Tell me what?'

'Just hang on a little while longer,' Olly pleaded, going to peer down the corridor.

'Gee, fellas, don't be sad,' Georgy said. 'It'll work.'

'Is your mother really nuts?' Riley asked her in a perfectly serious voice.

'Could be!' Georgy shrugged. 'Aunty Lois said she's a real flake. And *she'd* know!' She started into a nursery jingle. 'This little piggy went to market…this little piggy *stayed home!* Listen, I betta go!'

'My God!' Olly moaned.

'I'll come with you as far as the stairs,' Riley said, taking Georgy's hand.

'Good on yah, cobber!' Georgy mimicked many a stockman she'd heard. 'This is going to be the hard bit.'

Marissa was furiously blinking back tears. She rushed in front of them. 'What on earth are you talking about, Georgy? Is this some sort of plan you and your father have worked out?'

'Yeah,' said Georgy, with a big satisfied smile.

'But darling girl, it mightn't come off!' Marissa cried in despair.

'Yes, it will.' Georgy was full of confidence. 'Dad will grab me back in the nick of time. Come on, Riley. What is that thing you say?'

'Go forth and conquer.' Riley supplied, but he didn't smile. Like Marissa he was deeply worried.

Marissa wasn't prepared to let Georgy go like that. She hugged the child to her and kissed her. 'Be brave, little one. Things might turn out a lot better than you think.'

Georgy flung her arms around Marissa's neck, then kissed her cheek. 'I really *love* you guys!'

It was too much for the tenderhearted Marissa. Openly crying, she followed the children out of the door only to hear Tara's voice somewhere downstairs, building into a scream. 'I'm not *asking* you to be her father. I just want you to keep her.'

'Golly gosh they're having a fight.' Georgy swung her head up to Marissa, who acted at once. She bundled the children back into the bedroom. 'You don't want to hear this,' she said, her back to the door.

Georgy gave her a wry look. 'Maybe I do.'

'Well, you're not going to,' Marissa said, frightened of what Georgy might hear. Wasn't she frightened herself?

'Okay!' Georgy backed off, ambling across the room in a duck waddle making Riley laugh. 'We'll stay here with Olly. *You* go listen.'

'For heaven's sake, this is *private!*' Marissa protested.

'No, go,' Olly urged, backing up Georgy. 'It will

be all over soon. Just go and listen to what she has to say, love. We have to know.'

'What right do *I* have to get into the middle of a battleground, Olly?' Marissa asked in confusion.

'Because you care about Georgy, that's why! She missed out on her mother's love but she's getting plenty of affection from you and Riley.'

'Yes, Marissa!' Georgy cried, following the logic. She ran back to Marissa and squeezed her hand so hard Marissa gave a yelp. 'Hey, sweetie, that hurt!'

'Sorry.' Georgy rubbed Marissa's arm up and down. 'I'm very strong. I can catch really heavy things. Please go and see what's going on. I can see you're worried sick.'

'Very well.' Feeling like she was under orders Marissa walked to the door. 'Olly, make sure they stay inside.'

'Count on it!' Olly promised.

Holt and Tara had moved away from the entrance hall. The voices were coming from the direction of the study. Feeling she had no real right to be doing this Marissa stole down the staircase, repeating over and over to herself, 'Please, God, help us out.'

A second later, she fell back against the wrought-iron banister as Tara cried out with great bitterness. 'Honest to God I hate you!' More likely she still loved him, poor unhappy woman!

'And I'm revolted by your callousness,' Holt responded, his vibrant voice carrying along the corridor.

'You wouldn't tell Jack?' Tara sounded beaten and tormented.

It was Holt's turn again. There was fierce determination in his voice. 'One day maybe Georgia will *have* to know, but until the time is right, you're going to keep your mouth shut. And you can spare me the crocodile tears. The only person you've ever thought of is yourself and what *you* want. You won't be scoring any points over me telling Georgy I'm not her father. All you'll be doing is traumatising her. You don't care about her. You never did.'

Marissa slumped down on the bottom step like her legs had given way. She was profoundly shocked. Yet didn't it explain so much!

'I might have cared if she'd been a pretty child. A sweet little girl I could have dressed beautifully. A child I would have been proud to show off.'

'How could she be a sweet little girl with a mother like you?' Holt retorted cruelly. 'Georgy may not be a pretty kid, but she's got something better than mere prettiness. She's as smart as a whip. She's got intelligence and personality. I won't have her crippled. Try blackmailing me and I'll go to your family—I suppose they've long guessed anyway—and Jack Garner and tell them all the whole story. God knows why Jack wants to marry you, but he mightn't after I'm finished with him. He's already got three grown sons. He won't want to start up again.'

'And neither will I!' Tara gave a cry. 'As far as I'm concerned, one is more than enough.'

'You're deprived all the way, Tara,' Holt said with a touch of pity. 'You accept my ultimatum?'

Marissa hugged herself with both arms, trying to coil herself into a tight ball. She felt chilled to the bone. Ultimatum, what *was* it?

'I do, you bastard!' Tara sounded as if she was choking back sobs. 'All the pain and grief you've caused me. I loved you so much.'

'How the facts contradict it!' Holt gave a short laugh. 'What an unnatural woman you are, Tara!'

'If I am, there are plenty like me,' was Tara's reply.

'Ah, well…time to leave.' Holt sounded as if he had used up all his patience.

Instantly Marissa reached for the banister, pulling herself up, ready to tear up the stairs.

'I'll fly you as far as Longreach,' she heard Holt saying. 'You can catch a flight back from there.'

'Thanks a bunch!' A snort from Tara.

'We have nothing to say to one another.'

'It's that little bitch, isn't it?' Tara's vehement cry stopped Marissa in her tracks. 'The boy hiding behind her skirts. She's his mother all right. I suppose some guy raped her when she was a bit of a kid.'

Holt's voice was as hard as tempered steel. 'Marissa has no more given birth to a child than I fathered Georgina.'

Marissa couldn't bear to hear one word more. She fled, desperate for sanctuary. Holt McMaster had given Georgy his name. He had looked after her every day of her short life, but she wasn't his. Tara had not only betrayed her daughter. She had betrayed her marriage. Yet Holt had kept a child who wasn't his own, allowing Georgy's mother to go off and lead her own life. Clearly there was the chance of Tara's remarrying. Another rich man, Jack Garner and surely many years older than Tara? But who could care!

How far into the marriage did Holt realise the baby wasn't his? Clearly forgiveness hadn't been on his agenda. He had sought and received a divorce. There was no question he had a strong attachment to Georgy. He had taken over the role of nurturing parent, but basically—as it had always struck her—his manner with the child was more in line with that of an affectionate uncle. Far more affectionate and patient than her own uncle Bryan had been with her. Knowing his ex-wife as intimately as he did Holt had counted on his plan working. He must have discussed such an eventuality at some time prior with Georgy, relying on her sharp intelligence to pick up on when the plan was being activated. Georgia had become a pawn, but only her mother had been prepared to use her in the most destructive way. Clever little Georgia had committed the cardinal sin of being the daughter her mother had never wanted. It was pretty devastating stuff!

In the wake of Tara's departure, life went back to normal. Or normal on the surface. A child's potential for self-healing was truly marvellous. Now that the threat of Tara had been defused Georgia explained 'Dad's plan' to them from the beginning.

'As soon as he took my hand I *knew*,' she said. 'We had a sorta Morse Code. Do you know what that is?' She looked at Marissa.

'Of course she does,' Riley piped up. 'But it's an old, old system. It hasn't been used for years and years.'

'Dad used it, didn't he?' Georgy retorted amiably.

'It's four dots for *P. P* is for Plan. He pressed four dots into my palm so I knew straight away.'

'You're one smart kid!' said Riley admiringly.

The children had a marvellous time decorating the Christmas tree, an extremely lifelike balsam fir towering fifteen feet. It had been set up in the entrance hall—the library table had to be shifted—so they were able to make full use of boxes and dozens of beautiful baubles and Christmas ornaments accumulated by the family over many decades. Catherine was on hand to supervise, enjoying herself thoroughly, the tenderness of her expression at the children's excitement and enthusiasm, an eloquent indication of her inner peace.

The following day, Christmas Eve, the family was due to arrive. Christmas dinner on Wungalla was a well-established ritual. Holt's mother and stepfather were coming, his two sisters; Alex and her husband, his younger sister, Fran, who was bringing her current beau, his uncle Carson Holt, his mother's brother, and his extended family. In all, a party for twenty, which included four children, to be held in the formal dining room.

Not knowing what her *exact* place was; how the family would receive her, what might happen, made Marissa's feelings of nervousness grow. She

saw Holt every day. She was introduced to every
visitor who flew or drove into the station on the
annual pre-Christmas calls. It just so happened
most groups included a young single woman who
openly flirted with Holt. The comings and goings
were many. Obviously he wouldn't have any difficulty finding another wife and she had to take
that to heart.

*Wake up! Look at them. Look at you. Not the
same world.*

Endless gifts were exchanged. Where had they
all come from? She was conscious of being under
close scrutiny, but always invited to sit down with
Wungalla's visitors; morning tea, lunch, afternoon
tea, whatever it happened to be. She smiled and
made conversation, poised on the outside, but
worried she wasn't getting much feedback from
Holt. Sometimes she had the illusion he had con-
signed her to the wilderness. It was frightening the
distance he seemed to have placed between them.
But what was the alternative? A giant slide into a
sexual relationship? Leading where? A dismissal
was usually the way. These days she was more like
a mechanical doll, doing everything that was
required of her, unable to stop.

Catherine was a steadying influence. So was
Olly. All three discussed the Christmas menu at

length. Now that was enjoyable. There was no snow in the Outback. No traditional roast dinners, not in the heat. Fresh seafood was to be flown in Christmas Eve from the tropical North's teeming waters. Barramundi, Red Emperor, and the Gulf magnificent prawns and crabs. From the pristine chilly waters of Tasmania, oysters, scallops, salmon, and ocean trout. That, too, would be freighted in. There would be baked and glazed hams, cold chicken and beef, plenty of salads and accompaniments and three desserts, they had decided on, an almond tart with burnt honey ice cream, a passionfruit flan with spiced strawberries and a luscious chocolate pudding.

Olly's kitchen was a hive of activity and much merriment. The house girls were well used to Marissa's presence in the homestead now, looking up from their allotted tasks with big smiles whenever she came into the kitchen.

Each night, late evening, with the children long tucked up in bed, she stopped to admire the lit up Christmas tree. It looked so beautiful. At the same time it brought back memories of her childhood that she thought would endure forever. A family portrait. Her mother and father sitting together on the sofa watching a televised Christmas show, hand in hand, very much in love, while she lay on the floor in front of them, looking over her shoulder from time to time to join in their laughter at something funny. She remembered their two heads close together, two beautiful people, equally matched. She remembered her mother's long blonde hair, her father's blue-black, in stunning contrast.

How happy they had been then! How different it had all been with her uncle and aunt.

Marissa walked towards the tree, adjusting one of the exquisite glass baubles, ruby and silver, partially obscured by fir needles. This was the first time since her mother had died she had helped decorate such a splendid tree. She had bought a small one some three feet high for Riley the Christmas before and helped him arrange lots of little presents around its foot, but nothing like this!

'Oh, God!' she murmured aloud, not wanting to be drawn into a feeling of overwhelming sadness. Some of their presents, hers and Riley's, lay at the foot of this tree. Nice things she thought, all they could afford. Holt had found the time to fly them into the Alice so they could go on a shopping expedition. He hadn't gone along with them. He had attended a cattlemen's function for a few hours before picking them up at a prearranged spot and speeding them back to the light aircraft terminal.

'So what's the heartfelt sigh for?'

She knew the moment before he spoke he was there, so acutely were her senses attuned to his presence. She turned, her nerves sizzling. Even the brilliantly lit Christmas tree blurred away. Distressed as she was by the sense of alienation between them, she felt a perverse thrill at the note in his voice. It was very nearly...*tender.*

'I can't afford to think about it,' she said, looking at him, the dominant figure in her life.

'Remembrance of Christmases past?'

'Beautiful Christmases, yes. The images keep coming.'

'Even these joyful occasions open up wounds. My father's death was a tremendous grief.'

'I'm so sorry,' she said. 'But your family will be here tomorrow.'

'I'm looking forward to it.' She was wearing a very pretty blue dress, one with a gold thread. He had never seen it before. Mysteriously it deepened the colour of her eyes to violet. 'You'll like them.'

'More importantly will they like me?'

He gave a short laugh. 'Not everyone is like Tara. And Lois. You threatened them. That's why they reacted the way they did.'

'How could *I* possibly threaten them?' Marissa

moved closer to the base of the staircase. 'That's just plain crazy.'

'It's not crazy at all!' His tone was crisp. 'Why have you been avoiding me?'

Startled, her eyes flew to his. '*You've* been avoiding me!'

'Maybe that was wrong.' He held out an arm. 'Come and join me for a moment,' he said. 'I feel like a stiff drink.'

'Why exactly?' she asked.

'Oh…maybe because of *you*. Come along. You're quite safe.'

She hesitated a moment, deeply inhaling. 'Shouldn't we turn off the lights on the Christmas tree?'

'Don't you worry about a thing,' he said, dryly, taking her arm and leading her back to his study. Once there he shut the door. It was a large room like all of the rooms in the house, filled with superb equine paintings, books, trophies, a collection of antique guns, but he dominated it easily. 'The children have been enjoying all the excitement. So has Gran. In fact everyone on the station is caught up in the Christmas spirit. Why not *you?*'

Her heart seemed to be swelling in her chest, filling up her rib cage. 'I could be wrong, but I think you're angry with me.'

'Nothing of the kind,' he clipped off.

'Holt, *please,* that's not true. Maybe *angry* is the wrong word. *Disappointed* in me?'

His coal-black gaze was unreadable. 'When you're doing such a fine job? You've even got Georgy into the swimming pool.'

'She *will* be able to swim.'

'I'm sure of it.'

'You needed me to trust you and I didn't.' Marissa stood there, unaware she was holding her breath until he answered.

'I guess there's that,' he admitted. 'Sit down. Can I get you anything? A cognac to help you sleep?'

'A mineral water will be fine.' She made a big effort to calm herself. She had enough fire in her blood.

He took a bottle from the bar fridge, poured the contents into a crystal tumbler, then handed it to her.

'Thank you.' She was so nervous her mouth had gone dry.

'I would think angels have radiant, blue eyes, wouldn't you?' he mused. 'And they probably dress in blue robes.'

Her eyes rose to him slowly. 'I don't know any angels.'

'Surely your guardian angel brought you here?'

He poured himself a single malt whisky, adding a little water.

She dipped her head. 'You've been very good to us, Holt.'

He sat down behind the desk, raising his glass to her before taking a mouthful as though he really needed it. 'Besides, angels always turn up at Christmas time, don't they?'

Beneath the banter there was tension in the room; tension so tight at the very next half turn it could snap. 'Can you please tell me something?' Marissa asked.

He gave her a slight smile. 'Now that depends on what it is.'

She ploughed on. 'Do you still want me here, or do you really want me to move on?'

'And what gave you that idea?'

'Please answer, Holt.' There could very well be heartbreak in store for her. To love was to lose. That had been her experience of life.

He raised his glass to his mouth again. 'Why, is it giving you sleepless nights? If so, you're not the only one.'

'Is it because you kissed me and wish to God you hadn't?' she asked painfully.

He stared back at her, realising he had forgotten the kisses of every other woman he had ever known. 'There are worse things than getting kissed, Marissa.'

Her hand moved in agitation to push back her hair, a loose dark cloud around her face. 'Don't for a moment think I read too much into it.' Might as well let him off the hook.

'You mean you're just not in love with me any more?' his voice mocked. 'Come on, sweet, so gentle Marissa. *Answer.*'

She stood up, placing her glass very carefully on his desk. 'I see you're in a tormenting mood.'

'Sorry, that's *your* department.' He rose, as well, coming around the desk to her, looming very tall.

'I hurt you. I know that.' Her heart was beating much too fast.

'Maybe I want to hurt you back?' He closed a hand around each side of her face.

She should have pushed his hands away, but she didn't. The excitement was *colossal!* She knew this man wanted her. She wanted him but a huge gulf yawned between them. She had to remember that. She was here in the capacity of governess to his daughter, who was *not* his daughter. Of recent days she thought he had intuited she *knew.*

'Do you know how beautiful you are?' he asked, his voice deep and low.

If she was she revelled in it, for *him.*

Her lips parted, an invitation not to be missed. He took it, his mouth catching up hers. It was ravishing. Almost beyond bearing. Everything and everybody were blotted out, except *him*. Not another thing in the world mattered except assuaging the hunger. What she felt was so overwhelming not even the word *rapture* could cover it. If he had set out deliberately to seduce her, it was *exactly* as if she had accepted her fate. The only trouble was, once she had given him her body, could she ever get her heart back?

However much she yearned for him, Marissa somehow found enough control to pull back before she was entirely lost. 'I should go!' Breath ragged, she lay a staying hand against his chest.

'You have to get past me first.' His arms were locked around her, his down-bent gaze intense.

'And what then? Do we find our way to your bed? Surely you have a few scruples about making love to your *daughter's* governess?'

He reacted on the instant, letting go of her. There was a hard note in his voice she hadn't heard before. 'You *know*, don't you?' His expression, so ardent a moment before, had turned grim.

'Know what?' She was circling him in a dance.

'Don't waste my time,' he warned.

She looked into his brilliant dark eyes, searching for the right way to explain herself and gave up in despair. 'It's not how you think, Holt.'

'Damn right it is!' he rasped. 'You were listening in on my argument with Tara?'

She tilted her chin. 'It's a wonder everyone wasn't listening in,' she said sharply. 'Tara was *yelling*. Even deep voices *boom*. Please, just let me explain. Georgy was anxious about what was happening downstairs. She begged me to go and see.'

'So you crept up on us?' he asked in disgust.

'I hated having to do it. I never dreamed of what I might hear.'

'Why not?' he countered, a daunting figure. 'I've caught your blue eyes on me any number of times, full of censure. I wasn't your idea of a proud, loving father and you didn't do much to hide it. Well, now you know. But surely you had your doubts?'

'No! I swear it!' She shook her head.

'Neglected wife finds solace with a passing stranger?' he suggested bitterly.

'Please don't, Holt. Fire me if you want. What happened in your marriage is none of my business.'

'Yet you feel it in your heart, your head and right down to your toes?' he challenged. 'Tell me the truth. I think I have a right to know.'

'Okay…yes! I do feel it!' she burst out. 'Trying to ignore one's feelings doesn't make them go away. I never meant to fall in love with you. I never thought I had enough spare energy to fall in love. You were who you were. I was just someone desperate to find a job. I didn't do it on purpose. It just happened.'

'So I'm to believe you fell in love with me, yet you were afraid to trust me?'

'Believe me, I wanted to,' she cried passionately. 'But I let go of trust years ago. I couldn't look to anyone to trust. Anyway, why couldn't you trust *me?* You wanted to know all about my life, but you wouldn't let me in on yours. You got it all wrong about Riley. Don't you see, Holt, we were afraid to trust one another. Now it's all too late.'

'*Is* it?' He locked a hand around her wrist. 'You're here. I'm here. Who else do we need?'

It was her last chance to turn back. *Think. Think.* But the frustration was scalding.

'You want me to go to bed with you? Is that it? Is that how it's going to be from now on? Wait until the household goes to sleep, then I visit you?'

A hard glitter of amusement came into his eyes. 'Marissa, I don't really give a damn who does the visiting. I want you, *yes*. I've wanted you from the moment I laid eyes on you in the park. Surely you believe in love at first sight?'

His voice and his eyes were working their magic

on her. At the same time they were challenging. 'I believe in *lust* at first sight,' she said as though that was what she recognised in him.

'You sanctimonious little witch!' he jeered softly. 'What is it exactly you want, a proposal of marriage?'

She turned her head quickly, bit her lip. 'I won't deign to answer that!'

'But that's what you'd like?'

'No, I wouldn't!' Sad one minute, she turned turbulent. 'You'd make one hell of a husband.'

'That's if I ever give you the chance to prove it.' There was a taut smile on his face.

'Please, let me go, Holt.'

There was more than a hint of desperation in her voice. He responded. 'Sure.' Dropping her hand, he turned away to pour himself another drink. 'I'll never forgive Tara for what she did,' he said. 'I'll never forgive her for abandoning Georgy. At some time in the future Georgy has to be told the truth. Until then, you're not to speak a word to anyone.' His eyes locked on hers for a long moment.

'As if I would!' Marissa protested. 'Georgy adores you. She has taken her mother's desertion in her stride, but I think it would kill her to be cut free of you.'

'So, what to do?' he asked sombrely, his handsome features tight.

'Do what you've always done,' Marissa told him gently. 'Protect her.'

CHAPTER NINE

MARISSA had no need to worry about how Holt's family would receive her. She was met with instantaneous liking. Catherine had set the seal of approval on her; the rest of the family fell easily into line. Marissa's fluttery feelings of nervousness vanished. In fact their friendliness and apparent pleasure in her company made the Christmas stay among the happiest days she could ever remember. The family also acted as a sort of buffer between her and Holt. They were unfailingly courteous and pleasant to each other in company, while making sure they were never alone together. When she had first met him Marissa had thought Holt severe—no denying he still had his moments—yet he couldn't have been more relaxed around his family and his cousins' young children who were closer to Georgy than she had imagined. Riley, too, was taken up as a little person who had brought feelings of happiness and stability into the troubled Georgy's life.

'We really owe, you, Marissa,' Holt's mother, Rachael, who had warmed to Marissa by the minute—it was almost as though they had a previous knowledge of one another—lightly touched her shoulder. They were sitting beside the swimming pool watching the children romping in the sparkling water. 'I've never seen such a transformation in a child. I only wish the two of you could stay forever! Riley is such a dear little boy.'

Marissa, turning to meet Rachael's dark gaze, experienced an odd flash of recognition. Rachael meant exactly that, which meant, she, Marissa, had either blown her cover, or Rachael could read her extremely well. Did Rachael know Georgy wasn't Holt's and thus not her grandchild? Marissa having met the family had the feeling the older members *all* knew, but no one was prepared to talk about it. Too much anguish. And what of Georgy's response had she been told in even the most caring and sympathetic way? She might never get over it.

Marissa was to remember that Christmas vividly. The wonderful food, the conversation, the topics they picked on. There was talk well into the night, layers and layers of conversation, some serious, some sad, some personal, some just plain funny; Holt's sisters laughing helplessly at anecdotes Holt told from the past. He was clearly adored by his mother and sisters, something Marissa found deeply touching. What she didn't realise was, how much she was watching him as he was talking. It wasn't until much later Holt's sister Alex was to point it out.

When they left the morning after Boxing Day everyone fell into one another's arms, clutching and kissing until Marissa felt she loved them all. This had to be a time warp, she thought. A time detached from reality. No one had treated her like a stranger, much less a lowly employee. She and Riley had been included as family. It was totally unexpected, and totally disarming.

'You have a real talent for endearing yourself to people,' Holt observed dryly, studying her uplifted profile. They had watched the charter plane carrying his family back to Melbourne until it was no more than a speck in the sky. 'My family loved you.'

'And they're delightful,' Marissa said, not fully realising there was something special about herself.

'Are you going to disappear inside your fortress now they've gone?'

'Only if I have to.' Her soaring feelings got the better of her. She smiled into his eyes.

'Never cast me as the villain, Marissa,' he warned, turning his head towards the children who was running around the airstrip still waving. 'Come on, kids. Time to go home.'

Marissa's heart turned a somersault.

Home! If only!

Something far too perfect had to be ruined. Lois gave them four hours to prepare for her arrival. Understandably she had not, after all, been invited to Wungalla for Christmas, but she was spending a little time with her friend Sue Bedford on neighbouring Bedford Downs and staying on for the Bedfords's New Year's party to which Holt had been invited as a matter of course.

Olly took the call. Lois wanted to deliver Georgy's Christmas present in person. 'Better late than never!' she'd trilled.

There appeared to be no way to stop her short of standing shotgun.

Once again Marissa had to set off in search of Holt, but by this time she was getting quite good at finding her way around the station.

'God damn it, I thought I'd got rid of her!' Holt quietly raged. 'Why didn't Olly tell her to buzz off?'

Marissa took her time responding. 'She wouldn't like to, would she? It's your place, not Olly's.'

'Lois is up to no good,' Holt said. 'Count on it. Those are two sick women.'

* * *

But Lois when she arrived couldn't have been nicer. Of course she had Sue Bedford in tow, which acted as a brake. Sue, a Junoesque figure with golden-brown hair, large brown eyes and clear lightly tanned skin, shot Marissa a long speculative look on introduction, not unfriendly. She had flown them over in the Bedford Downs chopper. Olly whipped up a mouthwatering afternoon tea, with delicious little sandwiches, freshly baked honey and sultana scones and her famous melt-in-your-mouth sponge layer cake from which Marissa excused herself. Lois hadn't come to see her after all, though she had greeted Marissa as if they were friends. The welcoming afternoon tea Marissa suspected was more for Sue Bedford's benefit than for Lois. Sue appeared to be well liked, because Catherine had come downstairs to greet her and stayed on for afternoon tea.

She found the children in the rear garden with Riley pushing Georgy higher and higher in the swing.

'Your aunt Lois wants to see you now, Georgy,' Marissa called. 'Stop pushing, Riley.'

Riley stopped immediately, throwing himself at Marissa and hugging her around her narrow hips. 'I think I've knocked myself out.'

'Then give it a rest,' she advised, ruffling his hair. 'Come along, Georgy.'

'I can't,' Georgy said.

That wasn't all that difficult to understand. 'Listen, sweetie, your aunt has brought your Christmas present. She wants to give it to you.'

'That's *her* problem,' Georgy said, not getting off the swing. 'I don't want it.'

'I think you should be polite, Georgy,' Riley said. 'You're nearly seven, you know.'

'Oh, okay then!' Georgy gave in, struggling to get off the swing. 'You've got to come with me, Riley.'

'She doesn't want to see *me,*' Riley pointed out aghast. He never wanted to see Georgy's aunt Lois again.

'Well, I'm not going by myself.' Georgy plonked down on the grass. 'She might start shrieking again.'

Marissa shook her head. 'That's not going to happen. She's brought her friend Sue Bedford with her.'

'Really?' Georgy brightened up. 'Akshully, I don't mind Sue. She talks sensibly to kids. She's another one in love with Dad, but she's smart enough to know he just *likes* her. Righto, let's go!'

Afterwards Riley had to commiserate with Georgy on her aunt's choice for a Christmas present. It was a beautiful and obviously very expensive bride doll, exquisitely dressed in full bridal regalia, standing nearly two feet high. Another little girl would have *loved* it—Marissa actually loved it—but Georgy *hated* it.

'For one thing she's got *blond* hair, just like my mother's,' she railed. 'And Lois's. I really dislike blond hair. And I don't like *dolls.* I'm too old for dolls. Why didn't she bring me some games or some books or some movie DVD's?' She fell back on the rug in Marissa's bedroom, staring up at the ceiling. 'This is my *worst* present ever! What's it supposed to mean? She's been trying for years to get Dad to marry her.'

'I can't think she meant *that,* Georgy,' Marissa said. 'Anyway you behaved very well.'

'That doesn't mean I hate it less,' Georgy said and started to roll onto the carpet. 'I'm going to be a very nice person like Riley.'

'You *are* a nice person,' Riley said. Georgy rolled back and patted him, clearly a sign of appreciation.

'Let's put the doll away and try the trampoline,' she suggested.

Marissa was sitting quietly reading, one eye on the children, Dusty sitting close by joining in the fun, when Lois found her.

'Ah, there you are! I didn't want to go without saying goodbye.'

'That was nice of you,' Marissa said, slipping a bookmark between the pages of her thriller and closing it. 'You've never been nice before.'

Lois nodded. 'Well, yes, but who could blame me?' She sat down in a companionable manner beside Marissa. 'Isn't that just the cutest thing?' she said, glancing towards the children. 'I see they've still got that damned yapping dog.'

'He's just having a good time,' Marissa said, un-ruffled. 'Better not speak too loudly though. I seem to recall Dusty doesn't like you.'

'Ugly mutts don't scare me,' Lois snapped.

'What about your sister? Doesn't *she* scare you? She scared me.'

'I don't find that at all surprising!' Lois returned loftily. 'You're nothing and no-one. You and my sister aren't in the same league.'

'Thank God for that!' Marissa only shrugged.

'But we have to hand it to you. Both of us want to express our admiration at the way you're going about trying to land Holt. A *huge* prize in any girl's language.'

'I'm not about to argue,' Marissa answered wryly. So the claws were out! She might have guessed.

'I had an affair with him,' Lois said, lying effort-lessly. 'It went on for quite a while.'

'That must have been the time it took for you to wake up. I presume you're talking about a dream?'

'No dream!' Lois cried sharply, another big lie. 'As it turns out he's not the man for me.'

'Now that's more like it,' Marissa said, hoping Lois would simply pick up and go.

'Georgia isn't his, you know,' Lois continued, almost conversationally.

That piece of information delivered so callously would have rocked Marissa once. It didn't then. 'All that matters right now is she *thinks* she is,' she said quietly.

'So you know?' An astonished Lois leaned forward to stare into her face.

'Your sister has a very loud voice,' Marissa ex-plained dryly. 'I couldn't help but overhear. Why are you telling me this, Lois?'

Lois's supercilious eyebrows shot up 'Excuse me, my dear. We're not on an equal footing, so no Lois for you. I've never told a soul before about Georgia. It's a family *secret*. Tara got drunk at a wedding and had it off with some guy in the band. It was the *worst* mistake of her life. He meant nothing to her. She was missing Holt. He was out of the country somewhere. She was madly in love with him but she couldn't miss out on sex. She lost him. Just like that!' Lois snapped her fingers. 'I don't intend to tell anyone else about Georgy, on one condition.'

'He marries you, for better or worse?' Marissa asked ironically. 'Worse, I'd say. The only thing that needs to be cleared up is would he actually marry his ex-wife's sister?'

'I've checked,' Lois said very coldly. 'He can.'

'But *won't!*' Marissa was debating whether or not to whistle Dusty over. 'I'm sorry, Lois. Unrequited love must be very painful.'

Lois stiffened. 'Well, as I said before I *can* celebrate our affair. It was great while it lasted. My friend Sue Bedford has always carried the torch for Holt. She looks so much better since she lost weight. We all know Holt is going to remarry some time soon and Sue is in the running. We would back Sue. Holt needs an heir for one thing. Georgy doesn't count.'

'What is it you're trying to say?' Marissa asked, not bothering to hide her disgust. 'I'm sure it involves a threat of sorts?'

Lois threw up beautifully manicured hands. 'No threats, just a simple request. Move on. I'm not suggesting you steal away in the dead of night. But find some reason why you ache to be back in your home town. I would die of shame if I'd had a deadbeat drunk for a father who shacked up with an Islander, wasn't it? You see, we know all about you, Ms Devlin. The boy mightn't be yours, but the game is up! You must be out of your mind if you've allowed yourself to think you'd make Holt a suitable wife. Not with *your* background, my dear. People talk. We'd make *sure* they did.'

Marissa recoiled. 'Now aren't you a horrible creature,' she said. 'Forget what you want to do to me. The real crime is you're prepared to risk traumatising your own little niece.'

Lois gave her a contemptuous look. 'That won't happen if you *go.*'

Marissa stared back into those cold green eyes. 'You're not worried I'll take all this to Holt?'

'If you love him you'll shut up like a clam,' Lois snapped. 'In fact, if you care anything about the McMaster family, you'll pick yourself up early in the New Year and head off. Invent a boyfriend you can't get out of your head. Say you're sick to death of Outback living, the heat and the isolation. Say whatever you like, but if you want to ensure the McMaster and Devlin family skeletons stay in the cupboard, you'll go. We're not cruel people. We're prepared to help out financially. I expect you'd be glad of a handout?'

Marissa struggled to contain her anger. 'Believe me I'm thinking more about giving *you* a back-hander,' she said. 'Or I could call Dusty to speed you on your way.'

Lois snorted at the empty words. 'Think about it. You can't afford to waste more of your life. Holt may well fancy you—God's knows you're pretty—but there's no way in this world he would consider *marrying* you. You can't be such a fool as to think otherwise? Stick around and you'll only increase your misery.'

'Well, you'd know all about that, wouldn't you?' Marissa countered, her nerves snapping back to control.

'I'm trying to be a friend,' Lois said. 'How does twenty thousand sound?'

I don't believe this!

'Not near enough,' Marissa said.

Lois sighed. 'Okay, we'll go as high as twenty-five.'

'Thirty-five, and you'll get lucky,' Marissa said, staring straight ahead.

'What a mercenary little bitch you are!' Lois sneered. 'Thirty!'

'You people must be seriously wealthy?'

Lois nodded. 'I would have thought that was obvious.'

'Maybe I should make it more then,' Marissa said.

'Don't push it! That's the final offer,' Lois stood up, smoothing the creases out of her trousers. 'Your credentials are real. You can get another teaching job and a minder for the boy. Just make your story good. That's all we're asking for the deal to go through. Holt *must* believe you *want* to go.'

Before she left, Sue Bedford went out of her way to invite Marissa along to the Bedfords's New Year's Eve party. 'You must come. You should come,' she said and looked off to Holt with what could only be described as a look of adoration.

Marissa had the odd feeling Sue thought in issuing the invitation she was ensuring Holt's attendance. Even Lois was smiling sharply no doubt working out another way Marissa might be hurt. Holt, however, stunned them all—Marissa in particular—by saying he had accepted his sister Alex's invitation. Marissa had been invited along, as well.

A look of total disbelief came over Lois's thin face, but Sue rallied, swallowing her disappointment. 'Well, give her my love,' she said, kissing Holt's cheek in farewell. 'Nice to meet you, Marissa.'

'Was that just an excuse?' Marissa detained Holt long enough afterwards to ask. One of the station mares was running with a brumby mob and he was out to get her back.

'Not at all.' Holt paused at the base of the steps, his akubra pulled down over his eyes. 'The invitation is real. I just haven't told you about it until now.'

'But Alex never said a word?' She could hear the suspicion in her voice.

'I told her not to.'

'Thank you,' she said dryly. 'I can't go, Holt. The children need me.'

For some reason that made him smile, a flash of white in his darkly bronzed face. 'You don't think you're being just a little bit overly protective? Olly is here. So is Gran. So are Bart and his wife, indeed the entire station staff. The kids will survive a day or two without you.' He turned to move off.

'This invitation is *real* isn't it?' She ran down the steps after him.

He halted so abruptly she almost slammed into him. 'For God's sake, what else could I have in mind?'

'I won't fit in. I *don't* fit in, Holt,' she said, looking away.

His dark eyes glittered and he swore gently beneath his breath. 'What in hell are you talking about?' He was studying her closely, seeing the upset she was trying to hide. 'What has Lois been saying?'

His intensity scared her for a minute. 'Nothing!' She shook her head, a tremor running through her.

'Look,' he said, 'Do you want to come along on the chase? Blow out the cobwebs. I want the mare back. We'll pick up a few of the brumby's harem, as well. We don't want him. He's a rogue. I can give you five minutes. Well?' His eyes pinned her.

But Marissa was already moving. Anything to seal off the depression her conversation with Lois had triggered; the letting go of hope. 'Yes, yes!' she called and ran back into the house to change her clothes.

They arrived at the Bailey Melbourne mansion to a house filled with people in a festive mood, already well into celebrating the New Year. It took Marissa some time to catch her breath. She was taken under Alex's wing—told how beautiful she looked—and introduced to so many of their friends it was difficult to take it all in. Big as the house was the main reception rooms, entertainment orientated, were crowded. The Baileys were obviously very popular. Guests spilled out onto the spacious loggia, another outdoor living room, and the lush grounds beyond, with their rose gardens, banks of pink hydrangeas, large swimming pool and cabana and a playing fountain. Fran

McMaster, arriving, caught sight of her and broke away from a group to come through the crowd to embrace her.

'Marissa, isn't this wonderful! You've come!'

Was it all planned without her?

Alex's husband, Steven, couldn't have been more welcoming. One would have thought everything was working splendidly, only Marissa couldn't forget Lois's threat. She knew perfectly well Lois and Tara would have no hesitation in lashing out. They would do everything in their power to shame her but that was nothing to the injury that could come Georgy's way. How could they use a child as a pawn without being left with feelings of self-loathing?

Later it seemed to her she was taken up by everyone else *but* Holt. Not that he ignored her. He was always within a few feet of her but he obviously had obligations to be attentive to all his sister's and her husband's friends who were making such a fuss of him. Strangely it didn't dawn on her people were making a fuss of her, as well. In particular, the *men,* always interested in a pretty woman, but only one man existed for Marissa.

Many a dancing partner reached for her, wanting to know all about her, laughing off her comment, 'Just a governess!' as inconsequential.

'A governess who looks like this?' She was held away a little so her partner could get the full picture.

She knew she looked good. Physical beauty had a certain cachet. She had spent a good deal on her dress. How had that happened? She knew she couldn't afford it. But she had wanted to look as lovely as possible. She wanted her appearance to cry out to Holt, *'Look at me!'*

It was almost impossible to extinguish that ray of hope that continued to flicker inside her.

Holt was there, his hand on her partner's shoulder. *'My* turn, Toby, I think!'

'We'll catch up again later, Marissa,' said Toby, smiling broadly.

His arms closed around her, the marvellous re-assurance of his body. 'How does it feel to be belle of the ball?'

She lifted her dark head to him. 'I'm not, you know,' she slowly answered.

'You'd have fooled me.'

'I lost count of your glamorous partners,' she said. How many swooning women had there been?

He didn't answer straight away, manoeuvring them towards the loggia. 'Counting, were you?'

'You're going to remarry, aren't you, Holt?'

His laugh was unexpected. 'We can carry on until then. Hey, that was a joke!' His down-bent gaze was on her lovely poignant face. 'Of course I'm going to remarry. I could only do better than the first time.'

'That sounds very cynical.'

'A broken marriage makes one cynical,' he said, pulling her nearer as other dancers encroached on their space. 'Look up at me.'

She raised her eyes feeling as though her bones were turning liquid.

'There's something worrying you, isn't there? I've learned to read you very well.'

'Our experience of life is said to be retained in the eye,' she said. 'You have a full family life. A loving family. The talk is Steven will be a future Prime Minister. That means Alex will be second in line to the Governor General's wife.'

'Second in line will make her more than happy.' He shrugged. He looked incredibly handsome in formal dress. Enough to take her breath away. 'So where is this going?'

'My father was a brilliant lawyer,' she said. 'He had a great future.'

'Take it easy, Marissa,' he said, his hand smoothing over her back, much of which was bare. She was wearing a silk taffeta halter necked dress in a dark rose with an organza ruffle around the deep V of the neck. She wore no jewellery other than her mother's treasured pendant earrings that had been made up to her father's design; different coloured precious stones, diamonds at the top, sapphires, amethysts and peridots, at the end of the sparkling waterfall, a golden pearl.

'I've lived through some pretty bad times,' she said.

'Time to let go now,' he said. 'The bad times are over.'

She couldn't speak.

At the first stroke of midnight guests turned to the others around them with bright, expectant faces, hopeful that the New Year being ushered in would be better and more peaceful than the last! There was always that promise. There were lots of hugs and kisses, linked hands and voices raised in the age old rite of singing Auld Land Syne.

Marissa caught momentarily alone at the French doors felt an arm close around her waist drawing her back into the loggia. Her breath quickened and her heart sped up. She had no difficulty knowing who her captor was. Her bones knew it. Her blood knew it. The very air around him signalled is presence to her. He had come.

He turned her, staying very quiet as he did it. Then she was staring upwards into his brilliant dark eyes. 'How everything has changed!' she whispered, unaware of the beauty and poignancy of her expression. 'You've changed my life! I want you to know that.'

He pressed her slender body against him, desperate to pick her up, carry her away, keep moving, but mindful he was at his sister's party with crowds of guests celebrating around them. 'A very happy New Year, Marissa *mia,*' he murmured, then he lowered his head. His mouth caught up her mouth, kissing it, wanting to keep kissing it, while she kissed him back bringing all her heart and maybe her soul into it. She was so soft, so lovely, so *wonderful* to be close to.

It wasn't a long kiss—not that it mattered—there were people all around them doing just that, but the depth of emotion, the just *you* and *me,* filled Marissa with such rapture she felt lighter than air. She could fly if she wanted to! She had wished for this special moment between them marking the start of a new year. It had happened in the most perfect, intensely moving way.

The party continued long after they left which was around one-thirty or a little bit after.

'What about late lunch tomorrow?' Alex suggested when she saw them to the door. 'Barbara and Rex are coming. They'll be so happy to see you, Holt and to meet you, Marissa. They couldn't be here for us tonight. Rex's mother got in first.'

'I'll ring you,' Holt promised, kissing her cheek.

The hired white limousine stood out the front, the driver waiting.

All the way back to the hotel where they were staying neither said a word yet the air between them was scented not only with her fragrance that suggested exquisite flowers, but an intense and expanding intimacy.

In the lift taking them to the suites at the top floor Marissa's mind was in a panic. One minute she was prepared for the most momentous sexual encounter of her life, the next she was struck by the searing thought it could quite possibly destroy her. She had seen more than enough evidence of Holt's popularity with women. He would quickly get over her, if the truest thing about their relationship was, he simply *wanted* her. What he would require in a *wife* might be something else entirely. Tara, neither a successful wife nor mother, had nevertheless moved among the highest echelons of society. Holt's sister Alex, a beautiful person, seemed poised to move into a position of even greater eminence.

Any direction I take I stand to get hurt.

Tara and Lois had made it their business to find out all about her. More precisely about the tragic decline of her father; the fact that he had fathered a child by a young woman he had never married, a young woman of uncertain origin. She, herself, had nothing to hide. She had no dubious past that could come back to haunt her. She had worked hard and led a blameless life. But then wasn't there that line about the sins of the fathers? Her poor father had been more sinned against than sinning.

The lift doors opened silently. They stepped out into the empty corridor. He reached down, took hold of her nerveless hand, then wrapped her to his side. 'Where do you want to go, your suite or mine?' His tone was low and very intense, matching his expression.

Her mind was too crowded with conflicting words to answer. She pictured them embracing, falling on the bed… Already she was swimming towards him, head dizzy.

'Okay, I'll decide,' he said in his most clipped voice. 'Yours. You might feel more comfortable there.'

Comfortable! How could she be comfortable when she was unravelling like a torn sleeve.

They were barely inside the grand suite before

all her resolutions crashed. She was *on fire* for him, her flesh so hot she felt chafed.

His mouth plundered hers as though he had to have her that very moment. 'Are you safe?' he rasped when they came up for air. 'Is it a safe time for you, Marissa? I have protection.'

'We don't need it.' Both of them had known this was going to happen.

A groan came from somewhere deep in his throat. He shifted his hands to unzip her dress. It slithered off leaving her naked except for a tiny pair of lace briefs. He was steering her towards the bed, all the while kissing her, caressing her, his mouth tasting of champagne. One arm reached back to wrench at the quilted satin bedspread. He flung it away.

She was down on the bed now, exposed to his sight. The bedside lamplights fell over her in a wash of gold. His fingers began to move with great sensitivity over her bare skin, circling, feathering, absorbing the satiny texture of her white flesh; caresses that had her arching her back off the bed. She could hear her own tortured breathing…

He bent his head whispering her name…he was trailing kisses from her mouth to her throat to her breasts, taking her erect nipples with exquisite gentleness between his teeth…lapping them with the tip of his tongue, suckling them so she felt a hot piercing sensation slice through to her groin. Her hands flailed, then reached up to claw at his back, her nails catching at the fine fabric of his jacket. She didn't want *anything* to divide her from him.

He felt the same. He pushed up, leaving her momentarily bereft. His face taut with a deep concentration, Holt began stripping off his own clothes until he stood naked, a living sculpture. His skin was a dark bronze all over, evidence of a lifetime of cleansing plunges into Outback lagoons. He was looming over her, staring down at her with eyes so brilliant they might have been torched from within.

'You're so beautiful, Marissa. You're so *many* things!' He lay down beside her, thrilling her, his body so strong and splendid, so *warm.* 'These curls are as soft as feathers,' he murmured, the fingers of one hand spearing through her hair, holding her face to him. 'I'm going to keep you with me for ever!'

A visible tremor shook her. *When we're doomed to say goodbye?*

But what was to stop her from having him tonight? Even if her heart was torn from her she would have this memory for ever!

Living happily ever after only happened in fairy tales

Take your rapture where you can!

His tongue slipped down over her body while his hands cradled her hips. He made no move to strip her of her lace briefs until they grew damp and she was left gasping, the most intimate area of her body quivering and pulsing, wanting so much more attention. He lifted her slightly from the bed and eased them off.

Lights were flashing in her head, an illusion of scintillating Catherine Wheels. Warnings or not of bodily peril, she made no attempt to stay him.

His hands and his mouth were leaving imprints all over her body. He was carefully turning her determined to know every last little thing about her. She was going places she had never gone before... going to places only he could take her. No one before or after him would know her like this.

'I can't see how any other woman could be as beautiful as you!' he muttered, his voice almost gutteral in his passion.

She tried to say something; tried to catch her breath, but it was hard when she was balanced on the extreme rim of ecstasy and agony. 'You'll find someone,' she whispered, moving her knees wide apart so he could come between them.

And then: *Delirium.* 'Not after *you!*' he declared, before burying himself inside her like a rod of flame.

* * *

She didn't know how long it took for her to come back to earth. More pride to him he had recovered quicker. He was resting back against a couple of pillows, his arm wrapped around her holding her in to his body. He was wearing something around his neck that glittered, a white gold chain. Something was attached to it nestling into a dark whorl of his chest hair.

'My God!' he breathed. 'You are the most fantastic woman!' He kissed the top of her head. 'Wherever you took me, I have to go there again.'

She lifted herself up so she could stare into his marvellous face. He looked *exultant*. There wasn't a better word for it. He leaned forward and kissed her mouth. 'I have to thank you for being *you!*'

She couldn't help it. Tears came into her eyes.

'Hey?' His voice was deep with concern. 'I didn't mean to make you cry.' He kissed her again. 'You're not sorry, are you? I didn't hurt you? I know I got a bit rough at one time, but having you overwhelmed me. Marissa, what is it?' He took hold of her hands.

'What is it you've got around your neck?' she asked, her heart pounding.

He kept a hand on her shoulder loosely. 'What does it look like, my love?' With his other hand he put a finger beneath the object suspended from the chain. It was a glorious ring, a large perfect sapphire, flanked by diamonds. 'I'm certain it'll look a lot better on you.' He twisted the chain around, seeking the clasp. 'Here, you find it. After all, it's yours!'

'*Hush!*' She put her fingertips against his mouth. Making love they had been sealed off from the world. Now reality struck. 'It's not possible, Holt.'

His brilliant eyes flashed. 'You're not going to tell me you've got a husband?'

'Don't joke.' She turned her face, then lay it against his chest.

'No joke, Marissa,' he said and his voice was very firm. 'I love you and I want to marry you. This is your engagement ring. Are you going to tell me you don't want it?'

A wave of pain crossed her face.

He tugged at her long silky curls. 'Marissa, speak to me for God's sake.' Effortlessly he turned her over so she was lying on her back with him poised over her.

'I don't know where to start,' she said raggedly. The intensity of his regard awed her.

'Take it slowly. Let it out. You love me, don't you? You couldn't let me love you the way I did if you didn't.'

'I do love you,' she said, not sweetly, or sadly, but *fiercely,* her blue eyes ablaze.

'So, what's the big problem?' he asked in consternation. 'Why is there torment on your face? I just know it has something to do with that damned Lois. I knew that right away. What has she said to you?'

He shouldn't press her. 'Nothing that isn't the truth.'

His expression, so triumphant, grew dark. 'Is it something to do with Georgy? You don't have to worry about that. I've taken care of it. Tara won't be fool enough to open her mouth. Depend on it. My having custody of Georgy suits her right down to the ground. You've seen that. Lois would be a fool to get in the middle and cross her sister. Something happened, didn't it?' The beautiful ring swung hypnotically before her eyes. What a miracle he should love her!

'My background isn't pretty, Holt,' she said painfully.

'Oh, don't talk such rubbish!' His answer came right away. 'Bad things happen in every family. You're talking about your father here and his decline into self-destruction?'

'My father, even when he went missing, dominated my life. If I married you—' She broke off, choking on the words. 'Don't you see, Holt, my background would impact on yours. It would be like holding up a scandal to the world.'

His hand slid around her throat. 'I wouldn't care if you were the most scandalous woman in the world, I'm not letting you go. Has Lois attempted to blackmail you in some way?'

She could hardly say yes. 'Of course not!'

'Which means she *has*. I might have known it would happen. They're good at blackmail those two.'

Marissa shuddered and he lowered himself in the bed, pulling her close. 'Start from the beginning. Tell me *everything* Lois said. I'm not letting you out of this bed until you do. You're *my* woman and you must learn to trust me!'

CHAPTER TEN

ALEX came to the door, arms outstretched, a warm welcoming smile on her face. 'Come on in,' she invited, kissing each in turn. 'Marissa, don't you look lovely! You're positively *glowing* and after such a late night!' Alex's fine dark eyes slipped laughingly towards her brother's.

'That's right, Alex. You can congratulate me,' he said, turning on his wonderful smile. 'Marissa has made me the happiest man in the world.' He drew Marissa to him. 'She's consented to marry me.'

Alex looked thrilled but not all that surprised. 'I thought she might!' she crowed, holding her two hands up and pressing them together.

'Like my ring!' Roses in her cheeks, Marissa extended her hand for Alex's inspection.

'It's *gorgeous!*' Alex's voice rose with excitement. 'It couldn't be anything else but a sapphire with *your* eyes. This is marvellous news and the timing is great.' Her glance shot back to her brother. 'Does Gran know?'

Holt nodded. 'You were second in line. She's thrilled. She told me she's not going to join the angels until after we've had our first child. Marissa and I will break the news to the children when we get home. Is Fran coming?'

'She's here already,' Alex said, half turning her head. 'Come through you two. If this isn't the most wonderful way to start off the New Year! I couldn't be happier for you both.'

In Jack Garner's mansion high above magnificent Sydney Harbour, a small crowd had gathered for drinks. A maid appeared to tell Mrs McMaster, fiercely glamorous in a Chanel original, she was wanted urgently on the phone.

'How very odd!' said Tara, getting up from her chair and patting Jack's densely muscular shoulder.

'Take it in my study, dear!' Jack Garner called, indicating to a circling waiter to top up the glasses, before turning back to his friends and launching into a very funny yachting yarn.

Lois, who had been invited along—unthinkable to leave her out—felt a cool shiver of presentiment. She had been wondering for days if the girl would forsake all wisdom and go to Holt with her story. Holt would know immediately Tara would never go against him if it meant Holt would expose her for what she was. A she-devil. Tara was desperate to marry poor old Jack, a good fifteen years her senior, with the start of a potbelly, but as rich as Croesus.

Jack finished his story and Lois joined in the gusts of alcohol-fuelled laughter though she hadn't heard a word. She was on tenterhooks until Tara returned. She had gone a bit overboard giving the governess the impression she and Tara were in on the threat together. The fact of the matter was Tara had nothing to do with it. No way Tara could have been persuaded to part with even a teeny portion of $30,000. Tara had modelled herself on their father who still had the first dollar he had ever made.

Tara caught up with her a few minutes later, dragging her aside. 'How many bloody times have I wished I never had a sister!' she hissed. 'What a fool you are, Lois. That was Holt on the phone. He's in Melbourne with his fiancée and you know who *that* is! They're having lunch with darling Alex.'

'So?' Lois asked. Surely this wasn't the best time for Tara to blow her top.

'So I explained your little ploy had nothing *whatsoever* to do with me, though you had the colossal hide to set me up! Of course he didn't think for a moment I was involved. He knows me too well. I assured him I'd have a word with you, my dear. You're not very bright, are you?'

'And you're brilliant?' Lois sneered, though her lower lip trembled.

'You bet I am!' Tara narrowed her eyes to slits. 'It's over, Lois. Face it, you dim-witted dummy. The delectable Ms Devlin has achieved the one thing neither of us could. She's got Holt to love her. No miracle, she rather impressed me if I'm going to be honest. Anyway it's absolutely essential Holt has custody of my love child. Got it?' She put her fingers around Lois's arm and twisted hard.

'Got it,' Lois moaned in physical and mental anguish. She had been frightened of her sister ever since they were kids.

Marissa and Holt returned the following afternoon flying in to Wungalla as the fiery desert sun was sinking low in the sky. Olly and the children were there at the airstrip to greet them.

'Couldn't keep them at home,' she explained. 'They were too excited.'

Riley rushed to his sister, snuggled into her side. 'Finally you're home!' he made it sound as if they'd been on a world trip.

Georgy dancing up and down beside him, dragged Marissa's head down to her level and gave her a resounding kiss. 'Say, you look great! That's a new outfit, isn't it?' Her keen eyes gave Marissa a thorough inspection. 'Oh—oh!' she said. 'What's *that* on your finger?' She started to strut around Holt and Marissa.

'What is it? Let me see.' Riley was lightly frowning. 'Goodness, it's a—'

'An engagement ring!' Georgy cried. 'Well, of course it is. You two guys are engaged.'

'Are you, Marissa?' Riley asked, sounding uncertain.

'We are, Riley,' Holt said. 'I hope that meets with your approval. I love your sister with all my heart and I'm more than ready to love you. Georgy, of course, has had my love since she was half a minute old.'

'And I love you, too, Dad!' Georgy announced, for once overcome.

Olly standing to one side gave a deep satisfied sigh. 'Congratulations you two! It's truly wonderful things have ended this way. You've picked a rare young woman, Holt,' she said, earning herself a kiss on the cheek from Marissa.

'And don't I know it!' said Holt.

'So that makes me what?' Georgy twirled to look thoughtfully at Riley who was now wreathed in smiles. 'Your stepsister?' She moved back to claim his hand.

'I guess so!' Riley looked to the adults for confirmation.

Georgy shook her head. 'No, that can't be right!' she said. 'Surely you haven't forgotten you're going to marry me when we grow up?'

Above their heads the adults exchanged amused glances, not without a moment's wonder if that could indeed happen.

The tenderhearted Marissa thought she would hold a picture of the two children together forever in her heart.

We can take up our lives now and live them to the full!

Life up to that point hadn't been easy for any of them, but in Holt she had finally found the passion and deep connection her loving nature craved. Holt had made the world a safe place not only for her but for Georgy and Riley.

For Holt who had thought he would most likely never find that *one* woman, his soul-mate who would make him *whole,* Marissa had come as a revelation.

Love is the greatest transformer of them all he thought. It can make the best of all possible worlds out of what was once wreckage. Even as he thought it the love of his life turned to him and gave him her glorious smile.

On a wave of exultation he bent his head to kiss her. 'Love you,' he murmured.

'Love *you!*'

Holt straightened and lightly clapped his hands. 'Right! Pile into the Jeep and I'll get us all home.'

Home! Isn't that exactly what everyone wants?

MILLS & BOON PUBLISH EIGHT LARGE PRINT TITLES A MONTH. THESE ARE THE EIGHT TITLES FOR JANUARY 2008.

———— ❧ ————

BLACKMAILED INTO THE ITALIAN'S BED
Miranda Lee

THE GREEK TYCOON'S PREGNANT WIFE
Anne Mather

INNOCENT ON HER WEDDING NIGHT
Sara Craven

THE SPANISH DUKE'S VIRGIN BRIDE
Chantelle Shaw

PROMOTED: NANNY TO WIFE
Margaret Way

NEEDED: HER MR RIGHT
Barbara Hannay

OUTBACK BOSS, CITY BRIDE
Jessica Hart

THE BRIDAL CONTRACT
Susan Fox

MILLS & BOON®
Pure reading pleasure

1207 Rom LP

MILLS & BOON PUBLISH EIGHT LARGE PRINT TITLES A MONTH. THESE ARE THE EIGHT TITLES FOR FEBRUARY 2008.

———————— ❧ ————————

THE GREEK TYCOON'S VIRGIN WIFE
Helen Bianchin

ITALIAN BOSS, HOUSEKEEPER BRIDE
Sharon Kendrick

VIRGIN BOUGHT AND PAID FOR
Robyn Donald

THE ITALIAN BILLIONAIRE'S SECRET LOVE-CHILD
Cathy Williams

THE MEDITERRANEAN REBEL'S BRIDE
Lucy Gordon

FOUND: HER LONG-LOST HUSBAND
Jackie Braun

THE DUKE'S BABY
Rebecca Winters

MILLIONAIRE TO THE RESCUE
Ally Blake

MILLS & BOON®
Pure reading pleasure